MW01196741

PRAIRIE JUSTICE

A NOVEL

BOOK THREE
THE BOUNTY HUNTER

G. MICHAEL HOPF

DEDICATION

TO THOSE WHO FIGHT FOR JUSTICE AND
PROTECT THE INNOCNET

"At his best, man is the noblest of all animals; separated from law and justice, he is the worst."

—Aristotle

PROLOGUE

MILKE HOMESTEAD, NOBLE COUNTY, OKLAHOMA TERRITORY

OCTOBER 2, 1893

Oscar Milke clenched his fists and slammed them on the table. He was tired of dealing with Franklin Hartford's relentless pursuit of his claim as well as the veiled threats. "I'm not making a deal, and that's that!" Oscar exclaimed.

Franklin leaned forward, the chair creaking as he moved, and smiled. "You're making a mistake."

"I need you to leave my house, now!" Oscar barked.

"Now, Oscar, that's not very nice," Franklin said. "Let's go back to the beginning and start this conversation all over again."

"I'm not signing my land over to you and that's that. I don't care what you're offering; I don't care how much you say you'll pay me or that you'll put me to work. I've worked long and hard, hell, my family has too, and we're not about to give this opportunity up to go to work for someone else again," Oscar declared, referring to the land he had recently acquired from the Cherokee Strip Land Run, the fourth of its kind in the Oklahoma Territory and largest to date, as approximately one hundred thousand people raced to secure a piece of land that day. Upon hearing the Cherokee Outlet was being opened to claim, he'd quit his job as a clerk in a feed store, packed his family up, and moved from their little town in Michigan. He had waited through the long lines to get his name on the roster, had waited even longer at the starting line, and rode like hell to find his little piece of paradise and claim it as his own. After so much sacrifice, he wasn't about to give it over to a man who hadn't followed the rules or abided by the legal parameters set forth by the local land offices and the Department of the Interior.

"Damn it, Oscar, my brother had this claim and those others before you and your friends did," Franklin growled.

"No, he didn't; his name isn't listed. Just because you or your brother squatted on this land a while ago doesn't give you legal claim. I went through the proper channels and stood on that line that day. I remember it vividly. I don't recall seeing you September 16, nope; you slipped in here and thought you could just take the land beforehand. Well, that's not how it works."

"You're either going to make this deal, or my brother will have to settle this another way," Franklin threatened. "You must understand that I'm willing to make generous concessions, whereas my brother, he has a different approach. I don't think you want to know what his is."

Oscar seethed at hearing another threat. "I said get the hell out of my house."

"Don't be a fool. You can deal with me. I'll work with you, but you have to make it a deal I can bring back to Allister," Franklin said.

"I'm not making any deal, not with you or your brother," Oscar fumed.

"Dealing with Allister is…well, he negotiates differently than I do," Franklin said.

The door burst open and in came Thomas, Oscar's thirteen-year-old son and oldest of his three children. "Pa, I need some help. One of the cows got out of the pen."

"I'll be right there, son," Oscar said.

Seeing Thomas, Franklin called out, "Come here, boy."

Thomas furrowed his brow, confused about why Franklin would want him to come over.

"Don't pay no mind to him. He's just leaving," Oscar said, waving his hand for Thomas to leave.

"Hurry, Pa," Thomas said, leaving as quickly as he'd arrived.

When the door shut, Franklin placed both elbows on the table and leaned over the table. "Oscar, I'll give you until tomorrow to make up your mind; after that I can't say what my brother, Allister, will do."

Allister Hartford was the older of the Hartford brothers and the most notorious. Rumors had circulated that he was a killer and cutthroat.

Oscar stood, towering over Franklin, and said, "I don't need a day to think about it. Now, out!"

The door opened again, and this time it was Agatha, Oscar's wife, coming in. "Oscar, your son needs you."

"I'm coming," Oscar barked. It was unusual for him to yell at his wife, but the situation with Franklin and Allister had pushed his limits of patience.

She pursed her lips, gave Franklin a scowl, and replied, "Do hurry. Your son could really use your help."

"You're a pretty little lady," Franklin said. He sniffed loudly and continued, "And ya smell good too."

"That's it," Oscar said, reaching down and grabbing Franklin by the collar. He lifted him up and hollered, "I said get the hell out." He dragged Franklin across the room and tossed him out the open door.

Franklin tumbled in the dirt, jumped to his feet quickly, and said, "That was a big mistake. You hear me?" Franklin dusted himself off and sauntered towards his horse tied up to a post in front of the house.

Oscar hollered, "Tell your brother I'm not making a deal and that's final. Go try your scam on another settler; it don't sell here."

Franklin mounted his horse. After settling into the saddle, he smiled and said, "Oscar, I hope you cherish your family, I really do."

"Agatha, go get my shotgun. I've had it with this bastard; it's time to put some lead in him," Oscar barked at his wife.

Agatha remained frozen in shock at how the conversation was on the verge of turning violent.

As Franklin backed up, he said, "I'll be seeing all of you very soon." He winked at Agatha then galloped away.

"What's going to happen?" Agatha asked.

"This is our land. I won't be swindled out of it," Oscar declared.

HARTFORD RANCH, NOBLE COUNTY, OKLAHOMA TERRITORY

Franklin knew exactly how his brother would take the news that Oscar wasn't taking any deal. A man of violence, Allister would no doubt lose his temper and ride out to negotiate the terms with a pistol in his hand; this was where he'd have to convince his brother that wouldn't work.

After years of being on the run, they'd come to Oklahoma Territory and squatted on the lands months before they were officially opened up for settlement. To the locals and the officials at the land offices, they were known as sooners and their claims weren't considered; something Allister nor Franklin would accept.

As Franklin tied up his horse, Allister emerged from the house. "Tell me he agreed to your terms, little brother."

"Give me one more chance. I'll go back there tomorrow," Franklin replied.

"No more chances. We tried it your way; now we do it mine," Allister growled.

"Allister, listen to me. We can't just ride out and gun down everyone who is occupying our land," Franklin said.

"Why not?" Allister asked.

"Brother, I've been with you since I can remember. I've defended you, I've fought by your side, and I'll always continue to stand by you. But after so many years being an outlaw, I don't think we should just go in there and kill these people," Franklin said, genuinely concerned about the blowback of such strong-arm tactics.

Allister walked up and placed his hand on Franklin's shoulder. He stared into his brown eyes and said, "I'm not moving; this is my land. I don't give a damn what some land office says or what this Oscar fella or the others have to say. They're on my land. I came here and claimed this from those savages. I know you have to remember when we first got here. We had to fight more than a few of them off. So after we make this place, this land, safe, then the government suddenly declares it open for settlement? Franklin, we already done settled it. I'm not moving, so unless you have something different, you best make that case, 'cause by tomorrow, I'm riding over to each one of those squatters and putting a round in them. I'll kill every man, woman and child."

Franklin understood Allister's frustration; heck, he felt it. When they'd settled the seven hundred acres six months ago, they hadn't seen nor heard from anyone. When word spread that the area was being opened, Franklin ventured down to the land office only to find out the land they were on was technically and legally still United States land, and when he went to sign up, he discovered they were behind another fifty-seven thousand other applicants with no chance of making a legal claim for the land they now occupied. It was then that he and Allister made the plan to stay put, allow the land rush to occur, then negotiate with those who claimed it. To date, they hadn't reached one settlement.

Allister waited for Franklin to give him a rebuttal,

but none came. "Be ready to ride out tomorrow, little brother."

"What about the law or the soldiers camped out nearby?" Franklin blurted out.

"The marshal and them soldiers are up to their necks with those damn savages to the west. They're not going to worry about a few families disappearing."

"You're serious. You want to kill all of them, including the children?" Franklin asked.

"The dead don't talk," Allister said. "If we're going to do this, we can't have anyone talking."

Franklin had been successful at keeping Allister at bay, but now it appeared he was out of options. If they were going to go out and start killing these families, they'd need some additional manpower. "We'll need some help."

"How do you mean?" Allister asked.

"If we're going to do this, let's do this right; let's hire some guns to come help us," Franklin explained.

"You're saying we hire some gunslingers or mercenaries?" Allister asked.

"Yeah. We hire a crew not from here to come in and clean up this mess. Once they're done, they move on; we get our land and that's that."

Allister pondered the idea for a second and said, "Fair enough. Get those hired guns in here by the end of the month. Make all the arrangements."

"Will do," Franklin said.

"And, Frank," Allister said, heading back towards the house.

"Yeah."

"I want the best, real gunmen, killers; I want this over quickly," Allister said.

Frank nodded, acknowledging he understood what he needed to do. He mounted his horse and rode for town.

CHAPTER ONE

OUTSKIRTS OF PARIS, TEXAS

OCTOBER 7, 1893

It had taken years, five to be exact, for Abigail to grow her reputation as one of the top bounty hunters west of the Mississippi River and a woman who always found her target. It was a hard-earned reputation for this twenty-three-year-old—filled with many hard rides, grueling fights and lonely nights—but she wasn't about to let Little Jim Avery change that. In fact, getting him would only cement the reputation she had worked so hard to get.

She had been tracking Little Jim for two weeks and finally found his hideout was a small house outside the little town of Paris. As if Little Jim wasn't causing her trouble enough, Abigail now had her arch competition, Grady Evans, hot on Little Jim's trail too. Just before riding out to the house Little Jim was holed up in, she'd gotten word that Grady was in town. There was no way she'd let Grady get Little Jim, no matter what.

Abigail rode up and promptly dismounted her horse, Cloud, an American quarter horse. Cloud had become her one true companion while out working a job. After the loss of her partner Dwight a couple of years before, she hadn't wanted another partner to ride with.

She ripped her Winchester Model 73 from the scabbard and took a position on a bluff that overlooked the house below. Here she'd have a good vantage point from which to survey and possibly take down her target.

The house sat by itself minus a small outhouse positioned in the back. For Abigail there wasn't a lot of guesswork; Little Jim was either in the house or out back. Tied up near the front of the house was a single horse. This told Abigail a lot; it meant someone was there. Now she just needed to confirm it was Little Jim.

Little Jim wasn't a man to take for granted. Over the past four months, he'd left a trail of blood and tears. From one town to the next, he'd lie in wait and rob the stagecoaches. He never stayed in the same area more than once; he'd rob the coach, then ride to the next town, reconnoiter, then rob again. To date, he'd made off with over seventeen thousand in cash and an untold amount in personal possessions from travelers embarked on the coaches. He was known to be a quick draw with his Colt and didn't shy away from using it either. As of now he'd killed eight men and wounded five; two of those wounded were women, as he'd shot carelessly into the coach one time outside Dallas. All of this meant getting Little Jim promised a healthy bounty of five hundred dollars and another notch in Abigail's belt. Fortunately for Abigail, the wanted poster stated *Dead or Alive,* and she preferred taking her bounties dead, not on account she liked to kill but because it gave her more flexibility. Plus hauling a dead body in was always safer than someone still willing to fight.

Abigail peered down on the house with her binoculars. Calling it a house was a stretch. It was very small, probably a single room with possibly a loft, and a single door was the only way in or out. Normally she'd reconnoiter a property, get verification her target was there, then wait until nightfall; but with Grady so close, she'd have to act outside her normal protocols.

The door opened.

Abigail focused in.

A man stepped out, a saddle in his arms. He marched to the horse and threw the saddle on the horse's back. He cinched it tight across the belly, stood straight up, and looked in her direction.

She examined his face carefully, looking for the facial scar Little Jim had that stretched from above his right eye down diagonally to above the left side of his lip. When he turned and faced her, she spotted it, as it stood out like a sore thumb. "Where ya going, Little Jim?" Abigail asked herself.

Little Jim spit out a wad of tobacco then disappeared inside the house again.

Abigail calculated the distance. It had to be three hundred yards, she guessed. If she had to take a shot from her position, she could and do so accurately.

Little Jim reappeared from the house, a rifle in one hand and what appeared to be a heavy sack in the other.

"Is that what I think it is?" Abigail said. A devilish thought came to her. *Why go for five hundred when she could get thousands?* She quickly dashed the thought though it was tempting. If she was one thing, it was honest; maintaining a high level of integrity was what mattered most to her. Anytime an inappropriate idea popped in her head, Uncle Billy's words would start booming in her head. *A man can lose many things—fortune, fame, a woman—but still live with dignity. Once a man loses his honor and reputation, he will always live in shame.*

The distant sound of a horse galloping hard hit Abigail's ears and tore her away from her thoughts. She looked in the direction it was coming from and spotted a lone rider racing towards the house. Abigail's eyes widened; she knew it was Grady. Her time had run out. She needed to secure the target and fast. She grabbed her Winchester, raised the long-distance rear sight aperture, put the butt of the rifle in her shoulder, and settled in behind it, resting her cheek against the rear stock.

Little Jim was still packing the saddlebags, unaware that sights were aligned on him and soon he'd have a .44-40-caliber round in his back.

Abigail focused on her sights and continued to squeeze. In her left ear she could hear Grady approaching fast. Her shot had to be perfect if this risky plan was to work. If she wounded Little Jim, this would turn into a standoff, with Grady interfering. The rifle fired, surprising even Abigail. She looked over the sights and saw Little Jim begin to walk towards the house. "I missed?" Abigail blared, shocked that she hadn't hit him or even close to Little Jim. She cycled the lever on the rifle, loading another round into the chamber, and took aim.

Little Jim staggered then dropped to the ground.

She hadn't missed. It was a good clean shot and

Little Jim was down.

Abigail leapt to her feet, ran to Cloud, and loaded up. After mounting her, she hollered, "Ya."

Cloud, always responsive, took off at a full gallop.

Down the slope of the hill and into the small expanse, Abigail rode. She spotted movement out of the corner of her eye and saw Grady as he emerged from a grove of small trees. She was farther away than him, assuring he'd get to Little Jim's body first.

As if her life depended on it, Abigail pressed Cloud to ride hard and she did. In no time they had cleared the distance and were in front of the house. Abigail jumped from the saddle and ran over to Little Jim, who lay face down, encircled in a pool of blood. She turned him over, praying she wasn't going to be surprised by it not really being Little Jim, to find she had gotten her man. "Got you."

Little Jim's eyes were wide open in a death stare.

"You live by the gun, you die by the gun," Abigail said. Grabbing him by his legs, she dragged him to his horse. The next part she hated only because she always ended up covered in blood. Bending down, she lifted his body into a sitting position and held him there. Now came the most difficult part, getting him from there onto the back of his horse.

Grady rode up fast, only pulling on the reins just feet away. "Damn you, Abby Sure Shot!"

"Day late…five hundred dollars short," Abigail quipped as she struggled with Little Jim's body.

"This is the third time this year you've bagged the

bounty before me," Grady snorted. He shrugged his broad shoulders and spit tobacco juice onto the ground.

"You're just too slow is all," she said, squatting down, wrapping her arms around his torso then deadlifting his body. She set him against the horse, but the horse wasn't having any of it. It moved to the side a foot; then gravity took over. Little Jim's body slipped out of her grasp and fell to the ground.

"Looks like you need help," Grady said, taking joy in how difficult it was for her to load up Little Jim's body.

"I'm fine. I do this all the time," she said, her tone showing how aggravated she was getting from the ordeal.

Grady dismounted and walked over. "I don't mind helping."

Abigail had managed to get Little Jim up again, gave Grady a look, and said, "You don't mind?"

"Not at all," he said, taking a bulk of the weight of Little Jim in his grasp then tossing him over the back of the horse. "My pa always said that men and women are different. This is one of those differences."

"I can do anything a man can do," she snapped back.

"I know you can, you're a very impressive woman and a great bounty hunter; but when it comes to upper-body strength, not so much. I mean, you must weigh just shy of—"

"Just shut up," she fired back. "But thank you."

"How about we join together, create a team?" Grady asked.

Abigail cracked a smile and replied, "Why on earth would I do that?" Taking a piece of rope, she secured

Little Jim's body to the horse.

"On account having a partner such as me will only add to your earnings, and I can help load up the bodies," Grady joked, a big smile stretching across his face.

"Didn't you say this was the third time this year I got the bounty you were going after? And refresh my memory, I don't recall it happening the other way around…ever." Abigail laughed.

"Now don't go and get high and mighty. Every man can have his good days and bad. You just happen to be on a streak is all," Grady said. "And look at this bounty; you're not getting paid five hundred on account you killed the bastard. If we were a team, we could have taken him alive."

"First thing, you're wrong about Little Jim's bounty, it's five hundred regardless. Only if I had a partner would I be getting two fifty," she replied.

"But most bounties pay half for them dead. Little Jim here was an exception," Grady said.

"Grady, tell me, exactly what was your plan? You were riding in here like a bat out of hell," Abigail said, genuinely curious.

"I knew you were either here or close, and I was willing to do whatever it took to get Little Jim before you," Grady answered.

"I can appreciate that," she said, walking to a trough of water. She washed the blood from her hands and wiped them on her trousers.

"Think about it, riding with someone else helps alleviate the workload, and it's nice to have a partner;

makes for less lonely nights," Grady said.

"There it is, you can remove a man from the pig farm, but the pig always remains," she countered, shaking her head in disbelief that he'd make such a stupid comment.

"I wasn't meaning like that. I meant, don't you get lonely out there? Hell, I do," he said.

"Get a dog, then, or go find a partner other than me," she said, walking into the house to look around.

"I don't want just any partner, I want to be your partner. I know it's been a while since Dwight died, and I thought you might be up for a companion to ride the trails with," he said, following her into the house.

She tore through the place but didn't find anything of value. Pushing past him, she headed back outside. "I'll tell you what, I will think about it. Okay, I just did, not interested."

"Give it serious thought. You know I'm good at this stuff. You just happened to have been better the last few times," he said, coming outside too.

"You're following me around like a lost puppy," she said, taking Cloud's reins. She put her left foot in the stirrup, turned towards him, and said, "Grady, honestly, I don't think you're a bad fella. I'm just not interested in working with anyone else." She mounted Cloud and turned her head to the right and trotted her over to the other horse and took control of it.

"What if I came to you with a job, something special, would you consider it then?" Grady asked.

"The job would have to truly be special," Abigail

said, turning both horses around.

"That's a yes, I heard it, that's a yes." Grady smiled.

"We shall see," Abigail said just before cantering away.

MILKE HOMESTEAD, NOBLE COUNTY, OKLAHOMA TERRITORY

Oscar looked at the group gathered in his house and smiled. Having numbers to fight against Franklin and Allister would come in handy, and when people were joined together with a common goal or purpose, they made for a force to be reckoned with.

"I'm happy to have you all at my table. It doesn't have to go without saying, but we've all worked very hard, sacrificed much to be here today. Terrence, I know you brought your family all the way from Ohio, and you, Robert, came from Vermont; that's a hell of a journey. But the question is why? So that we'd have a future, that's why. All of us have traveled vast distances, given up a lot, and were told that the land we were staking a claim on would be ours, period. None of us expected to have that claim threatened, our dreams put on hold because of two brothers who came here illegally. I for one won't stand for it, and I gathered you all here to see if you'll join with me to oppose them."

"Word is Allister is a killer, is that true?" Robert asked.

"I've heard the same rumors. It's hard to know," Oscar replied.

"Someone should contact the army at the fort and tell them about the threats we've received," Terrence blurted out.

"Even if we did, they won't do anything. They're busy dealing with the Indians to the west of us," Oscar said.

"Then what about the US Marshal in these parts, or getting the land office to do something?" Robert said.

"I've mentioned it to the land office. All they did was confirm that neither Allister nor Franklin had a legitimate claim," Oscar answered. "Other than that, they won't do anything."

"Then what are you saying we should do?" Robert asked.

"We stand up to them collectively. If they know they have to take us all on, there's a good chance they'll back down," Oscar said.

"The offer for my land was not bad," Robert confessed.

Concerned by a break in the solidarity of the group, Oscar asked, "Have you taken their deal?"

"Not yet, but the wife and I think it's a pretty handsome offer," Robert said.

"Working for a killer, living on leased land versus what is rightfully yours? How is that handsome?" Oscar asked, baffled that anyone would even consider surrendering the legal claim of their land.

"I've heard that others have sold, not to the brothers, but they've sold to others already," Robert said.

"I've heard the same rumors, but let me ask you.

Why did you come here?"

"For land," Robert replied.

"For land to then give or sell right away? Or do you want to work that land?" Oscar asked, pacing the room.

Robert lowered his head as he thought about his answer. "I came to work the land, for the opportunity."

"Then why give it away for a quick lump of cash and a promise of continued work. Who's to say he doesn't need your labor after you sign over your land. Who's to say he doesn't evict you the next day?" Oscar asked.

"I'll get him to draft a contract," Robert fired back.

"And if he breaks that? Who's going to enforce it? The same marshal who doesn't have time to even listen to us now?" Oscar asked.

"Then what? What do you mean about standing up to them? Are we to fight? I'm not a gunfighter, that's not who I am," Robert said.

"I can see that the idea of fighting isn't what people had in mind, but we have to be prepared to do it. I say we make an alliance, join forces; if something happens to one of us, it happens to all of us."

Confused glances and unintelligible comments broke out in the room, mainly from the women, who were gathered in the back.

"What are you saying?" Terrence asked, his arms folded in defiance.

"I'm saying that if Allister or Franklin does anything to you or your land, we come to your aid," Oscar replied.

"You're asking us to come help you if they come here and do something?" Terrence asked.

"Yes, that's exactly what I'm saying," Oscar said. "If they know they have to contend with us not as individuals but as a whole, I predict they'll back down."

"And if they kill one of us, then what? Do the rest of us go kill them?" Terrence asked.

Oscar paused before answering the question. He didn't want to take the conversation in a direction where he'd lose control of the narrative, and he wasn't advocating vigilante justice either.

"Yeah, is that what you're saying, Oscar?" Robert asked.

"I'm simply saying we stand together," Oscar answered, wanting to move past that specific point.

"But does that mean we'll go out and exact revenge if they do anything against one of us?" Terrence asked, pressing harder, his tone shifting.

"I'm saying we come together collectively and support each other. This will empower us and give the brothers pause. I truly believe once they find out we've come together and won't tolerate their threats or any actions from them, they'll back off."

"But what if you're wrong?" Robert asked.

"I won't be. I've found men like Franklin and Allister to be nothing but thugs who prey upon the weak," Oscar declared confidently.

"You're very sure of yourself," Robert said.

"What do we do about them on our land?" Terrence asked. "He's occupying prime parts of my claim. Do we just let him sit there?"

"Until things settle down, yes," Oscar answered. "We

need time is all. Once things get to an equilibrium, we'll be able to get the law in here. Right now, things are just chaotic everywhere, and land disputes are the last thing any marshal or colonel wants to hear about or deal with."

"So we just let them sit on our land?" Terrence asked.

"Yes, for now," Oscar said.

"Then what's the point of this so-called collective?" Robert asked.

"He thinks he can intimidate us. He won't if we're all together against him. Just let him be until we can bring this to a listening ear," Oscar said.

Robert and Terrence gave each other thoughtful looks.

"Are we in this together? Shall we make an alliance to combat whatever Franklin and Allister have planned?" Oscar asked. He looked at each face in the room, hoping to see their responses conveyed there.

"I like the sound of it, but I need to think about it more," Robert answered.

"Count me in," Terrence said, raising his hand, his earlier skepticism gone as he saw the value in solidarity.

Oscar didn't like hearing Robert's response, so he decided to do something unconventional and ask the wives. "Ladies, what do you say? Can we count you in too?"

Pamela, Terrence's wife, looked at Candace, Robert's wife, then gave Agatha a look, hoping to be reassured.

Agatha nodded.

"If we're going to do this together, then yes on one

condition," Pamela said.

"What's that?" Oscar asked.

Terrence looked at her and gave her an inquisitive look.

"Tell Terry to get the dynamite he stored in the house out of there," she said, scolding Terrence.

Several gasped.

"Is that true?" Oscar asked.

"It's not in the house, it's outside covered. I don't have a place yet. The shed is almost—"

"It's volatile and dangerous," Pamela snapped.

"I've got it to blast some boulders, and I don't have a dry place to store it until the shed is complete," Terrence said, defending himself.

Some crosstalk erupted concerning the dynamite.

Oscar raised his hands and said, "Everyone, we're not here to discuss dynamite. But, Terry, please do listen to your wife."

"As it pertains to all working together, I approve too," Candace said sweetly.

"Well, Robert, what do you say now?" Oscar asked.

"But I've told them I'm very interested," Robert replied.

"Tell them you changed your mind," Oscar said.

"I need to discuss this further with my wife," Robert said.

"I've given my approval to this alliance. I say no on selling now; we've risked too much. I agree with Oscar," Candace said.

"Very well, my dear," Robert said, smiling at

Candace. He faced Oscar and said, "We're in for sure."

"Gentlemen and ladies, I couldn't be happier. The outcome of this gathering has given me hope that soon the one obstacle in our way will be gone and we'll be able to utilize our land and begin the great work ahead without the threat of it being attacked or stolen," Oscar said.

PERRY, OKLAHOMA TERRITORY

Franklin waited patiently for the telegraph office clerk to return with the telegram. He burned with anticipation to read it, praying it was good news. If it wasn't, then he'd have to deal with Allister's wrath, something he always tried to avoid.

"Here you go, sir," the young clerk said, handing him the folded piece of paper.

Franklin snatched it from the clerk's hand, unfolded the paper, and immediately began to read it. A large smile stretched across his face.

"Good news, hey?" the clerk said, smiling.

"Yeah, very good news," Franklin replied, crumpling the paper in his hand.

"Sir, that will be—" the clerk said before being interrupted.

Franklin took a dollar coin and flipped it at the clerk. "Rest is yours."

"Thank you, sir."

"I'm expecting more to come, so you'll be seeing more of me," Franklin said.

"I'll have them here for you, sir," the clerk said.

"Good man," Franklin said and left the office. Outside, he spotted the Blue Bell Saloon, but before he took a step, he tempered his desire to go. If he showed back up at the ranch drunk, Allister would no doubt give him a tongue-lashing if not an outright beating, especially since he had such important news to deliver.

Allister rarely drank and had good reason. Their father was an abusive alcoholic who was so bad to live with it caused their mother to abandon them. Seeing how alcohol had affected his father, Allister would allow it to touch his lips on the rarest of occasions, but wasn't judgmental over anyone drinking until it became a problem.

For Franklin, alcohol was an alluring drug, one that he enjoyed to the point of inebriation. He could drink daily and would do so if Allister wasn't there to hold him accountable. He knew he had a problem and felt fortunate that Allister had his back; but sometimes he resented him.

"How do ya do, sir," a voice boomed behind him.

Franklin turned to find a well-dressed old man standing behind him. "Who are you?"

"My name is James Reeder, and I'm in the business of selling land," James said, smoothing out his thick gray mustache.

"I don't need any land, got plenty of it," Franklin replied.

"You do, which lot in town is yours?" James asked.

"Lot? I own just over seven hundred acres of land northwest of here. Gonna be setting up a cattle ranch,"

Franklin answered.

"A cattle ranch, hey?"

"Yeah."

"Cattle ranch means ranch hands, cowboys and the like. Those men will need a place to come drink. Unfortunately for them, all we have is that small little saloon right there, clearly not adequate enough to service all those people."

"Yeah, so what?" Franklin asked.

"You're a businessman, an entrepreneur, right?"

"I suppose I am," Franklin replied.

"Then give me five minutes of your time and I'll present you an opportunity that you can't say no to," James said, the tempo of his speech rising.

"I ain't got no interest in a new opportunity. I got enough as it is," Franklin said. He never liked being propositioned unexpectedly and always tended to shut people down.

"My kind sir, I beg you to give me just a few moments. How about you join me at the Blue Bell? I'll buy you a drink," James said.

The thought of a drink tempted him, especially a free one; but he held firm. "Listen, fella, I don't have time. I need to be headin' back."

"Look up and down the street. What do you see?" James asked.

Franklin did as he asked; he looked left then right. "I see businesses, buildings, tents, people, horses."

"Know what I see?" James asked.

"No."

"Opportunity, massive opportunity. What's missing in this town?" James asked.

Franklin again looked up and down the street. He scratched his head and said, "Maybe a new saloon. You did mention that place was too small."

"More than that, this town needs a hotel. It needs a large saloon but not just any, one that offers women, gambling, entertainment," James said, now using his hands to animate his story.

Franklin thought about what James had said, and he couldn't argue with him. Perry was new; it had sprouted at the same time the land rush commenced.

"Care to hear about my opportunity now?" James asked.

"I don't have much time, but go ahead," Franklin said.

"Good man, follow me," James said, waving for him to come with him.

The two made their way to the edge of town. James stopped and pointed towards vacant land. "That right there is the opportunity."

"Land? I told you, I have land already," Franklin said, annoyed.

"But not land in town. You see, my friend, this town will continue to grow, and those who have land in town will be the ones who get rich. Outside town there are tens of thousands of acres and it's all the same, nothing unique. You see, this land is unique, as it's right here. There are five lots available right now and I have them for a steal of a price."

"Oh yeah?" Franklin said, curious.

"Yes, sir, two hundred per lot. One thousand gets you all five lots, and you can build on them right away or you can hold them and sell them later, but I recommend you build a saloon there—one with a large gambling room, a hotel connecting, and has a dance hall for entertainment."

"Building all that will cost a fortune," Franklin grumbled.

"But it won't, as I've got some investors who I think will help. You secure the land; they will help finance the construction," James said.

"Finance?"

"They'll loan you the money and at great terms," James said.

"I'm not so sure about this," Franklin said, shaking his head. The irony for him was that for months, he'd been wanting to open his own saloon. However, each time he mentioned it, he was met with resistance, all because Allister felt he only wanted to run a bar so he had an excuse to drink.

"There's nothing to lose. You buy these lots, you control the northeast section of town," James said.

"There's nothing here. Town is back there," Franklin said.

"You need to have vision. Do you honestly think Perry won't ever grow? What you see here happened practically overnight. Now is the time to strike; now is the time to make your mark," James said, speaking to Franklin like a motivational speaker.

The words *make your mark* struck home for Franklin. He did want something to call his own, and maybe this was it.

"What do you say?" James asked, nudging him.

"I don't know. Can I think about it?" Franklin asked.

"Of course, but I won't hold these. Just yesterday I sold two lots in town."

"Do you have any more in town?" Franklin asked.

"No, sir, sold out; the future is here and these lots are priced right," James said.

"Can I buy one or two?" Franklin asked.

"Sure you can, but that's limited thinking. Why buy one or two when you can have them all and control this end of town?" James said, pressuring Franklin to go big.

"I think you're right about the saloon. I want to open one and—"

"You see, our meeting was fortuitous, destined," James chirped.

"I can buy two, okay. Yes, I'll take these two," Franklin said, pointing at the two closest lots to town.

"Only two? Are you sure?" James asked.

"I'm positive," Franklin said. "I'll take these two."

"Very well, let's go write this up," James said.

"How long will this take?" Franklin asked. A fear was growing inside him. He'd just committed to buying two lots for two hundred each, and he hadn't gotten Allister's approval.

James stopped and turned around. "Are you coming?"

Franklin didn't move; he was frozen to the spot. If

he followed the old man and made a deal, that could lead to trouble for him. Even in his head he could hear Allister yelling at him.

James called out again, "Well?"

"I'm sorry, I can't make any kind of commitment right now. Let me think about this. I'll be back in town tomorrow. I'll come find you and tell you then," Franklin said.

"That's fine. Just remember what I said; I can't hold any of these lots. It's first come," James reminded him.

"I understand, but I need to consult my brother," Franklin said.

"Ahh, I see, you need permission; I understand," James said.

Franklin gritted his teeth. "I don't need permission; I need to talk with him. He's my business partner."

"Business partner, of course. Well, come find me tomorrow; my office is next to the Blue Bell Saloon," James said. He turned around and sauntered off.

Franklin watched him go, all the while thinking of how he'd explain the opportunity to Allister without him thinking it was the same idea as before.

PARIS, TEXAS

Abigail coordinated the deposit of the bounty and left the sheriff's office with a smile on her face until she saw a grinning Grady leaning up against a post. "What do you want?" she asked.

"I want to talk about a partnership," Grady replied.

"We had this conversation," she reminded him, stepping off the walkway.

He swung around and said, "I've got a job you'll want to hear about."

Ignoring him, she kept a brisk pace towards the saloon across the street.

He called out, "It's an easy one too!"

"Then come with me and tell me about it," she replied, stepping up on the walkway in front of the saloon.

Grady ran across the street, dodging a couple of horses and a wagon. Reaching her, he said, "You want to partner up?"

"I didn't say that, I said tell me about it," Abigail clarified. "But only if you buy me a drink."

"Sure thing," Grady said, stepping past her and opening the swinging door of the saloon so she could go in.

She cocked her head and quipped, "Aren't you a gentleman."

"You might be tough as nails, but you're still a woman and due respect," Grady said.

Abigail quite liked hearing that. She entered the darkened saloon and stood for a second to allow her eyes to adjust.

More than a few cast her a quick glance with a couple shaking their heads at her, most likely due to her attire.

Grady walked up and said, "You get these hard stares wherever you go?"

"Yep."

"Go take that table there. I'll grab a bottle," Grady said, pointing to the left corner of the saloon.

"Root beer for me, but if they don't have it, I'll take a sarsaparilla," she said, not wavering from her position on consuming alcohol.

"Root beer? Is that a serious request?" Grady asked, not sure if she was fooling with him.

"I don't drink alcohol," she said.

"Really?" he asked, still showing surprise on his face.

"Yes, now go get the drinks before I get bored and leave," she said.

Grady hurried off and soon returned with a bottle of whiskey for him and a bottle of root beer for her with a glass of ice. He placed the glass of ice and root beer in front of her and said, "My son likes it with ice. I thought I'd ask, and they had some. Stuff is hard to come by."

"Hmm," Abigail said, savoring the root beer. She poured it over the ice, watched it fizz, and took a small sip. "It's good."

Grady relaxed into his chair and smiled. "You're like a big kid."

"What?"

"The second your lips touched that glass and tasted the root beer, your entire complexion changed. You looked like a happy little girl."

"That's nonsense," she said.

"I'm not making fun, I swear it," he said.

She took another sip, this time conscientiously trying to keep a stern look on her face.

"Now you're thinking about what I said," he remarked.

Placing the glass down, she said, "Tell me about this job."

"Yeah, right," he said, leaning forward and putting his elbows on the table. "I have an associate in Kansas City. He finds work for me, and he sent me a telegram yesterday about an easy job in Oklahoma Territory, outside a town called Perry. We're not hunting anyone; they just need some muscle to move a few squatters off their land."

"I'm assuming this might require using deadly force?" she asked.

"When does what we do never require that possibility?" he asked back.

"True."

"Anyways, he's looking for about four or five hired guns to go up there and run these people off," Grady explained.

"What does it pay?" she asked.

"They're paying per head. My man said it was a hundred per head, and they're providing food and shelter while we're there," Grady replied.

"When does he need us?" she asked.

"Yesterday, this is an urgent matter," Grady answered.

Abigail leaned back in her chair, folded her arms and thought. She was close enough to Dallas to make a quick visit to Madeleine, but the job sounded easy.

"Well, are you in?" Grady asked, his eyes wide with

anticipation of what she'd say.

"I'm not sure," she said.

"Oh, c'mon, ride with me. This will be fun," Grady said.

"Fun?"

"Yes, this will give us a chance to get to know each other better," he said.

"Who said I wanted to get to know you?" she fired back.

"Abby, you can't ride alone the rest of your days. This is easy money. All we're doing is running off a bunch of farmers and knuckleheads from back east. All you need to do is bare your teeth and yell and I bet they run off."

"Are you sayin' I have bad teeth?" she asked.

"No…wait, I didn't mean that. I meant give them a scary look," Grady explained.

"Now you're saying I'm scary?"

"Hold on, no, I didn't," Grady replied as he twisted in his chair.

She held a hard stare on him but couldn't for long. She burst out laughing and said, "You're so gullible. I was just messin' with you."

Grady shook his head and sighed.

Remembering he'd mentioned a son, Abigail asked, "I didn't know you had a boy."

Not expecting the question, he answered, "Yeah, he's eleven, lives with my sister in Hot Springs."

"Where's the mother?" Abigail asked.

"Died of typhoid," Grady replied.

"I'm sorry to hear that," Abigail said before catching a few obnoxious glances from the bar. She shot them a look back and hollered, "What the hell you looking at?"

The two men looked away.

Grady craned his head towards the bar and said, "What's wrong?"

"Those bastards were over there givin' me looks, no doubt not accepting me being in here and such," she replied.

"You really do get those a lot," he said.

"More than you know. I mostly ignore them, but sometimes they're just plain rude. I've been tempted more than a few times to just pull my pistol and whip them with it. But I put my annoyance aside and go about my business."

"People don't like change or things they don't understand, and you, my dear, represent both."

She cocked her head and glanced at Grady. She'd seen him a few times before over the past couple of years but never gave his sharp chiseled chin or blue eyes notice before. She liked the way he talked and his mannerisms. There was something alluring about him that had gone unseen before.

"And do you have any children?" he asked.

His question tore her away from her thoughts. "I, um..." she said, stumbling over her words. Images of Madeleine's tender face and curly hair popped into her mind.

Grady sat waiting for the answer, patient and earnest.

"It's complicated," she finally answered.

"Your child is with the father?" Grady asked, trying to guess.

"She's adopted and lives with a nice couple," Abigail replied.

"Oh, I see," Grady said. "What's her name?"

"Madeleine, her name is Madeleine," Abigail answered with a sweet smile.

"Beautiful name. My boy's named Joshua."

Needing to change the subject, Abigail asked, "How many squatters need to be moved?"

"Not sure, but does that mean you're in?" Grady asked.

"I'm thinking about it," she replied, taking a big gulp of her drink.

Grady poured himself a shot of whiskey and tossed it back. "Is there anything I can say that will convince you to go?"

"I just need to think it over is all," she said.

He scooted away from the table, took the bottle in his grip and said, "I'm staying at the Lone Star Hotel. I leave in the morning for Oklahoma. If you want to join me on this job, meet me downstairs in the lobby at sunrise."

Abigail nodded and said, "If I'm there, you'll know my answer."

Grady stood and stepped away from the table.

"Thank you for the root beer," Abigail said.

Grady tipped his hat and said, "Anything for a pretty lady. You have yourself a good night."

Abigail grimaced at the reference *pretty lady*. She

disliked the phrase when directed at her, but over the years had been growing more accepting, noting that it depended on who and why someone said it. Coming from Grady, she didn't take offense; in fact, she sort of liked it.

WICHITA, KANSAS

Owen Blake dismounted his horse, looked up and down the bustling street, and exhaled deeply. He was tired from a long day's ride and wanted nothing more than a hot bath, a bottle of whiskey, and a woman by his side. He spotted a boy headed towards a livery next door and hollered, "You there!" He placed his fingers in his mouth and whistled loudly.

Hearing the sharp whistle, the boy turned his head and called out, "You want me, mister?"

"You work for the livery?" Owen asked.

"Yes, sir."

"Good, then come take my horse and board him for the night," Owen said as he patted the dust off his trousers with his sweat-soaked hat.

The lanky boy ran up and took the reins of the horse. "How many nights, mister?"

"Just one, I'm leaving in the morning. I need him fed well and given plenty of water; oh, and give him a good brush," Owen replied, removing the saddlebags. He tossed them over his shoulder, grunting from their weight.

"Yes, sir," the boy replied, not moving from his spot.

"Well?" Owen sneered, seeing the boy standing and staring at him.

"That'll be two dollars, sir. We take payment up front. Mr. Burns says that's what we have to do," the boy said.

Owen cracked a crooked smile, smoothed out his thick black mustache, and said, "Payment up front?"

"Yes, sir. Mr. Burns does that on account of some people have come in and taken their horses without paying," the boy replied.

"Hmm, well, fortunately for you and your employer, I don't mind paying up front," Owen said, digging into his front vest pocket and removing two coins. He placed them into the boy's open hand and said, "Away with ya. I'll be around in the morning to get her."

"Yes, sir," the boy said, guiding the horse towards the barn.

Owen turned towards the saloon in front of him. A sign on the front read *WHISKEY, BEER, WOMEN, GAMBLING*. "My kinda place," he said out loud as he headed towards the swinging doors, only to be stopped when two men came bursting out. One hit the walkway while the other stood above him, fists clenched.

"I told ya I'd hit ya, I told ya," the man standing with clenched fists barked.

The man on the ground cowered in fear due to his vulnerable position.

Annoyed by the altercation, Owen stepped over the downed man and pushed past the other, grazing his shoulder on the way.

The man gave Owen a harsh look and growled, "Am I in your way?"

"As a matter of fact, you are," Owen answered as he walked inside the boisterous saloon. He spotted the bar and headed directly for it.

The saloon doors swung open again. This time it was the man whom Owen had just exchanged words with. "Where you think you're going?"

Ignoring the man, Owen proceeded to the bar, spotted the bartender, and called out, "Give me a bottle."

The bartender glanced at Owen then turned his attention to the man, who started towards Owen.

Owen looked in the mirror above the bar and watched as the man approached. "How about that bottle?" Owen asked the bartender.

Not wanting to be in the way of a gunfight, the bartender stepped away, as did several other people.

"You owe me an apology," the man hollered.

Owen didn't turn; instead he kept his eyes on the man in the mirror. By the man's sway, Owen could tell he was drunk.

"Are you listening to me?" the man spat as he reached for Owen's shoulder.

Owen quickly spun around. He pulled out his eight-inch-long sheath knife and placed it against the man's neck. With his left hand he held the man's right wrist, preventing him from drawing his pistol. "I don't know who you are, and I rightly don't give a damn. You might have gotten one up on that feller out there, but you're not going to with me."

The man could feel the sharp edge of the blade pressing against his throat. "Don't cut me," he said just above a whisper.

"I'm tired, and all I want is a few drinks, then a bath. I'm not here for trouble, nor do I want to kill anyone, but if I have to, I will," Owen said.

"I don't want any trouble either," the man said, quivering.

"Good, now get out of here," Owen said, pulling the knife away from the man's throat.

"Yes, sir," the man said and hurried out of the saloon.

Owen waited a couple of minutes just to make sure the man didn't find courage and come back.

The bar around him was silent, all eyes on him.

"Here's your bottle," the bartender said, placing a bottle of whiskey on the bar behind Owen.

Feeling comfortable, Owen turned, poured himself a glass, and cast a glance in the mirror just for good measure.

"You handled ole Hank with no problem," the bartender said.

Owen swallowed the shot and poured another. "I take it that Hank is the man to reckon with in this saloon."

"He likes to fight, that's for sure," the bartender said.

"He apparently doesn't like to die though," Owen said, tossing the second shot back.

"Will you be needing a room?" the bartender asked.

"I will and a woman. Can you arrange that?" Owen

asked.

"Of course I can. When will you be needing them?"

Owen picked up the bottle and looked at the contents and replied, "When I'm half done with this."

"I'll have them ready for you," the bartender said then walked away.

Pouring a fresh glass, Owen removed a piece of paper from his vest pocket and unfolded it.

The paper was a telegram, and on it was detailed his next job. He read it, pausing at the name Oklahoma. His mind went back to the last time he'd stepped foot there. He had been an officer in the army with the responsibility of relocating several hundred natives to a reservation in the Dakotas. The journey north could only be described as a bloody ordeal, and when it was over, he found himself court-martialed and disgraced. Returning would only bring up memories of his time there, but the money promised made the trip worth it.

"Your room is ready when you want it. Top of the stairs, last on the left," the bartender said, walking up to him from across the bar.

Owen didn't respond; he stared at the glass in his hand.

"Hey, buddy, you okay?" the bartender asked.

Torn away from his dark thoughts, Owen looked up and replied, "Ever kill a man?"

Shocked by the question, the bartender mumbled his answer, "Um, no, no, I haven't."

"It's a weird thing, it doesn't hit you until later. Once the adrenaline has worn off and you reflect on what's occurred. It's tougher when you do the killin' up close and personal, when you see the life leave the eyes of your opponent. You start to think about where they came from, if they had any children; heck, you begin to question yourself and if you had to do it."

"I'm sure it's a tough thing. Probably never gets easy," the bartender said, trying to add to the conversation.

"You're wrong, it does get easier, sorta like a callous on your hand. The more you do hard work with your bare hands, the tougher, more resilient your hands get. You no longer feel the pain of the labor. That's what happens to your soul after you've killed a lot; it becomes callous, unfeeling."

An uneasy feeling began to settle over the bartender. Who was this man standing in front of him?

"That feller Hank, he was lucky. I've killed men and women for less; heck, I've even killed children, and they did nothing but exist. They happened to be in the right place at the wrong time. Hank was damn lucky. You see, I didn't kill him because I felt some sort of obligation to preserve life, no, I didn't kill him because I didn't want the trouble that could come afterwards. I came in here to have a drink, get a bath, and get laid. If I had killed him, that would've possibly sidetracked all that."

"Okay."

"Hank is alive only because I didn't want to be inconvenienced. Now, isn't that something to think about," Owen said, tossing the full glass of whiskey back. He wiped his mouth and slammed the glass back on the bar. Snatching the bottle in his right hand, he asked, "Last door on the left?"

"Yes, sir," the bartender said, glad to see Owen was leaving.

"What do I owe you?" Owen asked.

"Fifteen dollars for it all, but I can collect later," the bartender said, just wanting Owen to go away.

Owen swished his fingers around in his vest pocket and removed a handful of coins. He counted as he deposited them onto the bar. "Seventeen, two dollars for you."

"Why, thank you, sir," the bartender said.

"And here's another five. I want privacy, you understand?" Owen asked.

The bartender took all the coins and replied, "Of course, I understand discretion. No one will know you're there."

Owen winked, picked up his saddlebags, tossed them back over his shoulder and, with the bottle of whiskey in his left hand, headed to the stairs.

HARTFORD RANCH, NOBLE COUNTY, OKLAHOMA TERRITORY

Franklin entered the house to find Allister talking to two workers they had recently employed for manual labor around their ranch. The trio was sitting around the table laughing.

"My brother is back. I hope you came back with

good news," Allister said.

Franklin held up the telegram and said, "I do."

"Being that you're here now, I can presume to thank you for not giving in to temptation at the sight of the Blue Bell," Allister said, showing how well he knew Franklin.

"I never gave it a glance," Franklin lied.

Allister turned his attention back to the two workers. "Go out to the north end of plot sixty-seven, that's the area I showed you on the map, and start fencing. You'll find all the material in the barn."

"Yes, sir," one of the workers said. The two got up and exited the house.

"You're having them begin fencing? That will most certainly be met with trouble from Terry Jones," Franklin said, referring to Terrence, who had legally claimed the land during the land rush.

"If that telegram has good news, we won't have to worry about Terry Jones or any of those other squatters for long," Allister said.

"I got him; he's coming," Franklin blurted out.

"Got who?" Allister asked, curious as to who could make Franklin so excited.

"Owen Blake is coming to work for us. He's in Kansas right now. I think we can expect him to arrive in a couple of days, maybe sooner," Franklin said, almost about to burst with joy.

"Who the hell is Owen Blake?" Allister asked.

"Only one of the most notorious army officers and gunslingers around these days. He's the army officer that slaughtered all those natives a couple of years back in Nebraska. Don't you remember the Bloody Creek Massacre?" Franklin asked, shocked that Allister hadn't heard the name. "His moniker is the Butcher of Bloody Creek."

"I heard of the massacre, just not about the man behind it, I suppose, but you were always more well-read and bookish than me. All I care about is that he can take care of our problem," Allister said.

"He will. I'm riding back into town tomorrow to see if there are any others coming, but he will most certainly be of value to us."

"Remind me what we're paying these hired guns," Allister said.

"One hundred per," Franklin replied.

"Even for the little ones?" Allister asked.

"Are you sure you want to kill the children too?" Franklin asked.

"Hell yes, I'm sure. I've never been more serious about something in my life than that. Weren't you telling me about ancient Rome and how anytime they assassinated anyone, they'd kill the entire family?"

"I remember telling you that," Franklin said.

"And why would they do that?" Allister asked, already knowing the answer.

"No witnesses, nor did they have to worry about some disgruntled child growing up and seeking revenge," Franklin replied.

"Sound, very sound; that's practical and wise, and we're going to do as the Romans here. So what are we offering for killing the children?"

"Fifty?" Franklin answered.

"Sounds a bit steep, but I'm fine with it," Allister said.

"Very well, but I haven't told them about killin' any children just yet. I didn't think that would sound tasteful in a telegram," Franklin said. "I'm hoping to get five men, so with Owen coming, we'll only need four more to handle the job."

"Good job, little brother," Allister said. "I'm proud of you."

"Thank you," Franklin said before looking down at the table and fiddling with his fingers.

"What vexes you?" Allister asked.

"I've been thinking, I'd like to take my money and open a saloon in town. They need another one, and once we're up and running, our men will need a place to go drink; why not have them go to our place?" Franklin replied.

Allister sighed.

"There's a terrific opportunity in town to buy two lots. We can build a new saloon, maybe even a hotel. We could have gambling and women," Franklin said.

"You just can't drop that idea, can you?" Allister asked.

"We have the money, and they're in need of a new place in Perry; we could do very well," Franklin said.

"That's if you don't drink all the inventory," Allister said, reminding Franklin of his bad habits.

"I've got that under control. It's been a while since

I've had anything to drink. I would just like something to call my own. This land, the ranch, the cattle—all of it is really yours. It was your idea and I came along."

"Frank, this is ours; we're brothers," Allister said.

"It doesn't feel like mine," Franklin said.

"Only because I make the decisions around here. A place this big needs a boss, a single boss. It wouldn't run smooth if both of us were making decisions, it would only cause problems."

"I understand that, so let me take some of my share from that last bank job and use it to open a saloon," Franklin said. The bank job was referring to the last time they'd held up a bank. It was a harrowing heist that had almost ended in them being captured.

Allister sighed again, this time louder. He was growing impatient with Franklin's requests to open a drinking establishment. "The timing isn't right."

"It's never right. Al, some of that money is mine; I should be able to use it for what I want," Franklin declared.

Allister clenched his jaw. He was on the verge of snapping at Franklin.

"What do you say, huh?" Franklin asked.

Taking a deep breath, Allister said, "You know something, you're right. Take some of that money and open your place."

"Are you serious?" Franklin asked, surprised by the sudden shift in Allister's thinking.

A large smile stretched across Allister's face. "No, I'm not serious. This is a horrible idea. Each time you ask,

I give you the same answer. You of all people owning a bar is the worst thing you could possibly do. There's no doubt in my mind I'd find you dead within six months. You would have drank yourself to death."

"That's not true," Franklin countered.

"Brother, it is. Have you forgotten about that time I found you? Do you remember? Because I do. You were so drunk you were lying in pig shit. You didn't have a cent to your name, and everyone in that hole they call a town knew you as the degenerate drunk who begged for money."

"That was one time," Franklin challenged.

"I found you once like that, but that was your life for months. If I hadn't pulled you out of the gutter, where would you be? Dead, no doubt. I saved your life, I gave you purpose, and now all you crave is to go back to that life. I don't understand it," Allister said passionately.

"I won't do that again," Franklin said.

"How do I know that?" Allister asked.

"Because I won't. I gave you my word back then after I got cleaned up. I won't," Franklin insisted.

"Brother, we're on the cusp of something great here. Soon those squatters will be off our land and we'll be set to grow a large and successful cattle business using the money from the jobs we did," Allister said.

Franklin crossed his arms and tensed his body. He found it difficult to look Allister in the eye, so he stared at the table.

Seeing Franklin's disappointment, Allister presented him with an idea. "How about we do this? Come next year, if we've grown enough, you and I both open this saloon. We'll find someone to operate it for us; then you'll have this establishment you so want."

"I want to run it," Franklin said.

"That's not an option. If you're there, the temptation will be too much. I fear you'll fall to it and end up in the ditch again."

Angered, Franklin bolted to his feet and spat, "You're just my brother, you're not my father. I can do whatever I want. Why you think I need to answer to you is nonsense. I'm my own man. I'll go take my share of the loot and use it however I desire."

Not one to be challenged, Allister slowly stood and stared Franklin squarely in the eyes. "You won't do anything but do as I say. If you don't, I'll…"

"You'll what?"

"Brother, I love you, but don't make me set you straight again," Allister said, referring to the time he had to beat him until he was unconscious.

Upset and unable to continue the conversation for fear of where it would go, Franklin walked away from the table and exited the house. Outside, he took a deep breath and exhaled heavily. He loved Allister, but sometimes, like now, he hated him with all his fiber. For him, it wasn't fair that Allister controlled every aspect of his life. He resented it, but what were his options?

Allister came outside. "I'm not trying to tell you how to live your life, I'm trying to save you from yourself."

"Al, I appreciate everything you've done for me. You were there when I was down on my luck. You found me after I left home and ended up in trouble. You brought me into your gang and gave me a place to call home. I realize I tend to like the bottle more than others, but I can assure you, I want to open this place to help us and to have something that's mine. I want to prove to you I can make it on my own."

Allister let Franklin's words marinate before he replied, "I want you to have your own operation, but not a bar, not something that will tempt you."

"How about giving me a chance?" Franklin asked.

"I have given you chances, and each time your lips touch the bottle, it's not long afterwards that you become someone else. You know this."

"Then I'm destined to just be your little brother. All I do is take orders."

"Not true, you're in charge of handling these squatters. You've been a good right-hand man when it comes to those jobs we pulled off. You're smart, capable—hell, sometimes I think you're cleverer than I; but the second the booze hits you, you change for the worst," Allister said.

"It won't happen, I swear it," Franklin pleaded.

"I can't take that chance, not now; we're too close to having everything we've ever wanted," Allister said, then removed a pocket watch from his trouser pocket and popped open the gold cover. "It's almost one. How about we take a ride to the west?"

"What for?" Franklin asked.

"Just to do it. It's our land; let's go see it," Allister replied, smiling. He took a leather pouch from his other pocket, opened it, and removed a small corncob pipe. He packed it with sweet-smelling tobacco and put the pouch back in his pocket. He swiped a match and lit the pipe. After taking a few puffs, he said, "Soon we won't have anything to worry about, little brother. Soon those squatters will be gone, and we'll be able to do whatever we desire with our land."

Franklin gave Allister a cockeyed glance. "This cattle ranch isn't everything *we* ever wanted, it's everything *you* ever wanted. Let's be clear about that," Franklin snorted and walked off.

CHAPTER TWO

PARIS, TEXAS

OCTOBER 8, 1893

Upon seeing the sunrise to the east and no Abigail in his presence, Grady knew the answer to his question was no. He gave the hotel clerk a nod and headed out the door with his saddlebags draped over his shoulder and his Winchester rifle in his left hand.

Paris was quiet at that hour. The only things on the street in front of the hotel were two stray cats, who quickly scurried away after seeing Grady.

He took a deep breath in and thought about staying a few minutes longer, just in case she was running late. It took him only a few seconds to decide that was wrongheaded. She had heard him, and if she was serious, she would've met him. Disappointed, he stepped off the walkway and headed to get his horse.

He entered the livery. Several oil lamps illuminated the space, giving ample light to see. "Anyone here?"

"Right here," a man cried out from the back.

"I'm here to get my horse," Grady said.

"Sounds good, boss. I'll be right there. I'm just helping the lady down here," the man replied.

Lady? Grady thought. He walked down the center aisle of the barn, stalls on both sides of him, until he reached the back of the barn.

The man had exited out the back door and was talking to someone.

Grady stepped out and saw Abigail standing next to her horse, Cloud.

"You're late," she said, her attention on her saddlebags.

"I'm late? I'm confused," Grady said.

She looked up and said, "You didn't wait long, did you?"

"No, I figured if you weren't there, you weren't coming. So, can I presume by your comments you are coming?" he asked, his face showing how shocked he was to see her.

"I am, but I wanted to make you think I wasn't up until the very last second," she teased.

"How did you know my horse was at this livery?" he asked.

She cocked her head and asked, "Is that a serious question?"

"Ah, of course, the cunning Abby Sure Shot can find anyone or their horse," he joked.

The livery worker walked up with Grady's horse and handed him the reins. "He's fed and rested, sir."

"Thank you," Grady said, handing him a few coins.

Abigail mounted Cloud and said, "I'm thinking we can get to Perry in three or four days if we ride hard, but now that I think about it, maybe five or six."

Grady finished getting his horse ready, turned towards her and asked, "Why five or six?"

"On account you're riding with me. I hear you're sorta slow in the saddle," she joked.

"You're just full of vigor and comedy this fine morning. You're not acting like the Abby Sure Shot I've heard stories about," Grady said, putting his foot in his stirrup and mounting his horse.

"Oh, really, and what have you heard about Abby Sure Shot?" she asked, genuinely curious about the rumors or talk.

"That she's tough as nails and meaner than a viper," Grady answered. "I never heard anything about having a sense of humor."

"I'd say all that talk is true, just not complete," she said. "Now, enough talk." Abigail pulled Cloud's reins and tapped her ever so gently with her spur.

Cloud responded promptly and began to canter.

Grady caught up and the two began to casually talk.

"What made you change your mind?" Grady asked.

"I could use an easy job," she replied.

"That's it? It had nothing to do with wanting to get to know me more?" he asked, his tone indicating he was teasing her a bit.

"I know all I need to know about you, Grady Evans," she snapped back.

"What? Okay, now you need to fill me in on the rumors you've heard about me," he said. Like her, he was sincerely interested in knowing what another bounty hunter had heard about him.

Abigail didn't reply.

After a few minutes went by, Grady again asked, "So

what have you heard about me?"

"I'm sure you already know. I'd hate to repeat it and only add to an already fragile ego," she quipped.

"You're relentless and sassy, aren't you?"

"Sassy is definitely not a word I've heard to ever describe me," she countered.

"Well, go ahead, tell me," he said, practically begging.

"Outside showing up just behind some other bounty hunters, I've heard you're a hard-nosed and determined man. I've heard that you're good with your hands and behind a rifle."

Grady nodded his approval of the way he was being described.

"And I've heard that you have a weakness for saving kids," she said, hoping he'd explain that rumor.

"I wouldn't call it a weakness, I'd call it a strength. Children are innocent, and it's up to us to defend and protect them. Anyone who would call it a weakness most certainly has some unresolved issues from their own youth or are moral degenerates."

"I've also heard that you have a Samson complex," she said.

"What in the hell is that?" he asked.

"That means you can fall victim to a pretty woman's graces," she explained.

"Who is Samson?"

"He was a figure from the Bible; supposedly he had incredible strength. He also had a weakness for women and gave away his one secret that would cripple him, the source of his strength, to a woman named Delilah."

"So you're saying I'm strong and like women? I'm fine with that." Grady laughed.

"I'm saying that we all have weaknesses. Best you know yours, so you can prevent it from destroying you," she countered.

"What's your weakness?" he asked.

"That's my business, not yours," she said and trotted ahead of him.

Grady caught up and said, "I promise I won't tell anyone."

"We're just starting our first job together. I don't really know you. I don't think I'm going to open up to you within the first hour."

"I also heard you were smart too; I can see that's true," he said.

"Can we move the topic away from us?"

"What do you want to talk about, then?" he asked.

"How about we just remain quiet and enjoy the beautiful landscape? Sometimes silence is bliss," she said.

He shot her a big smile and said, "Fair enough."

PERRY, OKLAHOMA TERRITORY

Franklin woke early and made for town. He had two tasks to accomplish, one being to check on any telegrams, and the second to talk to James again.

His first stop was the telegraph office. There he found the clerk and two telegrams. Like the day before, he could hardly wait to read the contents, and when he did, he found they contained everything he was looking for.

Two additional teams were en route, one from Texas and another from New Mexico Territory. He was impressed how far and wide his call for hired guns had gone. Within a week, he'd have his team assembled, and soon after that, he and his brother would be rid of the squatters and free to work the land they called theirs.

He paid the clerk and exited the office. Filled with promise and happy that everything was going his way, he went directly to a land office located down the street. He entered the small single-room office and found James sitting behind a small desk.

James looked up, removed a slim pair of spectacles from the bridge of his nose, and said, "You did come back. I pray you're here to make a deal."

"Are those two lots still available?" Franklin asked.

"Oh yeah, you're the gentleman who needed to talk to his business partner," James said.

"Are they?" Franklin asked again.

"Which ones were they again?" James asked, feigning ignorance.

"The ones at the end of the street; one sits next to the mercantile," Franklin clarified.

"That's right, yes, yes, they still are, but you never know, they go quickly," James said, once more applying his tried-and-true pressure sales tactic.

"I haven't gotten my partner to see the opportunity here, so I came to see if I can put something down, maybe a deposit of some kind, to hold the lots until I can get him to agree," Franklin said.

James stood. He smoothed out the creases in his slacks and replied, "Oh no, we don't take deposits; no, we sell them to the first buyer who has the funds. Now if you have those funds, I'll gladly get the title work going for you."

"I can't commit just yet, but are you sure you can't at least set them aside, maybe give me a week?" Franklin pleaded.

"Now, Mister...what's your name again?" James asked.

"Franklin Hartford."

"Mr. Hartford, I don't take deposits—"

"Whose lots are those? Let me speak to the owner. I'll make the deal with him directly," Franklin declared.

"Those lots are mine."

"Yours?"

"Yes, sir," James replied, standing tall proudly.

"Then why have you implied they were someone else's, and why won't you work with me on this?" Franklin asked.

"On account those lots are in demand and they'll sell soon. If I held deposits—"

Cutting him off, Franklin said, "I'll pay fifty more per lot. I'll pay you one hundred now and the two hundred each next week. If I don't buy, you keep the hundred."

"Hmm," James said, smoothing his mustache.

"What do you say?" Franklin asked.

"If you make it sixty per lot, you have a deal," James said.

Franklin didn't need a moment to think; he stuck out

his hand and said, "We have a deal."

James took his hand and shook. "Do you have the hundred now?"

"I do, but I need a contract, something signed showing we've conducted the deal," Franklin said, showing he wasn't about to be a fool and give up his money without legal proof. "When can you have that done?"

"If you'll give me thirty minutes, I can have it ready to sign," James said.

Franklin nodded and said, "I'll be back then." He exited the office feeling excited. He strolled down to the lots and stood staring at them. He walked onto them, knelt down, scooped up a handful of dirt, and held it in his hand. Running his thumb through it, he said, "You're gonna make me a lot of money." He dumped the dirt and turned to see the last man he thought he'd see, Oscar Milke, riding into town. He stood and watched until Oscar parked his wagon in front of the mercantile a few storefronts away.

Oscar jumped from the wagon and caught sight of Franklin. He scowled at him before quickly scurrying into the mercantile.

Franklin hadn't seen him since that day at Oscar's house. Filled with pride and cockiness, he strutted to the mercantile and walked in.

"I need a sack of beans…" Oscar said, pausing when he heard the bell ring on the door. He looked and saw Franklin.

"Anything else, sir?" the mercantile owner asked.

"Here's the list," Oscar said, handing him a piece of paper.

The owner of the store took it and walked off to get the supplies.

"Oscar Milke, a surprise seeing you in town," Franklin said, walking up to him.

"What do you want?" Oscar seethed.

"I never came back to see if you wanted to take that deal, 'cause my brother has decided to handle it his way," Franklin said, his hands planted firmly on his hips, one inches away from a Colt he had holstered on his right side.

"I'm not afraid of you or your outlaw brother. Just so you know, I've spoken with the other settlers, and we're united against you. You come after one of us, you're coming after all of us."

Franklin leaned towards Oscar. He was so close he could see the pores on his face. "You'll soon hear from us, and I can promise you, you'll rue that day."

"Go to hell. You'll never get one of us to vacate our land, never," Oscar declared, his temples throbbing with anger.

The mercantile owner returned but stopped when he saw the two talking aggressively. "I don't want any trouble in here, you hear me?"

"There's not going to be any trouble from me," Oscar said.

"Not from me either," Franklin said, giving the owner a smile. "I'm just in here saying hello and relaying a message."

"You both look like you're ready to fight," the owner said, making sure he stayed at a safe distance.

"I'll let you get back to conducting your business here," Franklin said, nodding to the owner. "And you, squatter, I'll be seeing you real soon."

"Go to hell, you hear me, go to hell," Oscar barked.

Franklin exited the store and headed directly to James' office.

"All done," James said. He waved Franklin over. "You sign here and date it."

Franklin looked down at the single-page document and paused before signing. He was about to embark on something that would cause so much discontent between him and Allister that it could literally sever their relationship. However, if he was to ever be his own man and claim something as his own, this was the time. He took the pen, dipped it in the inkwell, and scratched his name at the bottom of the page and dated it. "There you go."

James countersigned and said, "The funds?"

Franklin opened his jacket pocket, reached inside, and pulled out a small stack of paper money. Peeling off a single one-hundred-dollar bill, he placed it on the desk. "There you go, one hundred dollars as a deposit to hold the land for a week."

James quickly examined the hundred-dollar bill to ensure it wasn't counterfeit. Feeling it was legitimate, he said, "This officially concludes our business. Congratulations, Mr. Hartford, you have a hold on those lots, and I'll be seeing you in a week's time."

"I'll be here," Franklin said.

James offered his hand and said, "Nice doing business with you."

Franklin took his hand and shook it. "Thank you." He swiftly exited the office and exhaled deeply. A shiver coursed through him. He had done something but nothing so much he couldn't reverse it; but it gave him pride that he could stand alone and make a legacy for himself.

***

The encounter with Franklin disturbed Oscar. He liked to think he wasn't afraid of either him or his brother; but he was to a certain degree. The thing that aggravated him more than the brothers' endless harassment was the land office. It was as if they washed their hands of any disputes and expected people to handle it themselves. But what did that mean? Was he supposed to take Allister and Franklin to court? If so, where and how? Were he and the others supposed to find justice the old-fashioned way by forming up and running the two outlaw brothers off? The entire situation vexed him, and he sometimes questioned why he'd dragged his family to Oklahoma in the first place.

With his wares and supplies loaded up, he hopped on his wagon and was about to leave when a familiar voice called out.

"Oscar!"

He turned to find it was Terrence. He was across the

street in front of the blacksmith's shop.

"Howdy, Terry," Oscar hollered.

Terrence ran across the street. He looked in the back of the wagon and said, "Getting supplies, heh?"

"Yep."

"I'm just over getting some shoes made for my horses," Terrence said, pointing back to the blacksmith shop.

"Good seeing you, but I need to get moving; I've got a lot to do and…" Oscar said, pausing before he finished his thought. He removed his hat and shook his head in anger.

"You look a bit out of sorts," Terrence said.

"I am, Terry, I really am. I don't expect to get harassed when I come into town, but I do. I can't seem to get away from those damn brothers."

"Which one was it?" Terrence asked.

"Franklin," Oscar replied. "I've never met the other brother. Sometimes I wonder if he actually exists."

"You know, I haven't met him either. Maybe he's all made up by Frank to keep us scared, you know, all the talk about his rough and tough older brother," Terrence said.

"I'm not sure how long I can deal with this. What's next? I bring my family into town to go to church and they're there tormenting me? We need to do something about this, we really do."

"What are you thinking we should do? I thought we were going to watch each other's backs but not act offensively," Terrence said.

"Well, maybe we need to change our tactics, you know, be more direct; let them know we're not going to take their stuff," Oscar said, trying to clarify his thoughts.

"I should let you know that I found a trench dug and fencing on my land to the south. It was fresh, no doubt the brothers. It made me so mad I saw red. I tore it down and filled the trench back in. I happened to find it 'cause one of my cattle wandered off and got caught up in the wire; it cut him real bad. He'll be fine, but it just made me so angry. I thought about riding over there and giving those brothers a piece of my mind, let them know this is my land, but the ole wife talked me out of it."

"If I found that on my land, I would've probably ridden over there and shoved that fence up Franklin's ass," Oscar barked.

"You'd do that?" Terrence asked.

"Not exactly up his orifice," Oscar said, laughing. "But I'd tell him to stay off my land. I think we really need to take a stand."

"Hmm," Terrence said. He started to reconsider his reluctance to go over to see Franklin and give him back the fencing he'd taken down.

Oscar wiped his face with a handkerchief and said, "I need to be getting back. You be well and let me know if those bastard brothers do anything else on your land."

"You might want to ride out and check your land too," Terrence said.

"Good idea," Oscar said. "Well, good day to ya. Oh, and before I forget, did you get that dynamite stored safely?"

"It wasn't in the house and, yes, it's now down in the shed."

"Good," Oscar said.

"Tell Agatha I said hello," Terrence said, waving to Oscar as he pulled away. The thought again revisited him: maybe he should ride over and tell Franklin or Allister just what he thought and to remind them the land was his not theirs and to stay off it. Maybe Oscar was correct; they might need to assert themselves more than they had been doing and let the brothers know they weren't going to take any encroachment on their land lying down.

"Mr. Jones, your shoes are ready," the blacksmith called out from back at his shop.

"Coming," Terrence said, crossing back over the road. In the back of his mind, he couldn't stop thinking of going over to confront the brothers and make it clear that they were on his land not vice versa.

WICHITA, KANSAS

Owen lay back in the bed and exhaled deeply. He was having one of the better mornings he'd had in a long time, and it was because of Vanessa. He had missed his scheduled time of departure only because she wouldn't let him go. At first he found her persistence aggravating, but when she was done showering him with affection, his stubbornness had shifted to gratitude.

"What time is it?" Owen asked.

"Time for you to get this going again," she purred as she reached down between his legs to touch him.

"I can't. I need to go," he protested.

She scrunched her face and said, "That's what you said before, and now look at you."

He took her arms by the wrists and said, "You're a very special woman, that's for sure, and when I come back into town, I'll be sure to look you up; but I best be hitting the trail."

"Fine," she grunted, plopping onto the bed.

He sat up and swung his legs out of bed. His clothes were next to him, draped over a chair, with his gun belt hanging from the bedpost.

A loud commotion broke out in the hallway.

Vanessa sprang to her feet and opened the door, only to shut it quickly.

"What is it?" Owen asked, pulling one of his Schofield revolvers from the holster and cocking it.

"It's Hank, and he looks real angry," Vanessa said.

Hearing that name, Owen knew Hank must be coming for him. He turned to Vanessa and said, "Get over there, out of the way."

"What are you doing?" she asked.

"He's coming for me," Owen said.

"How do you—"

"Shut up and get over there," Owen barked.

Not saying another word, Vanessa did as he ordered.

Owen stood in front of her, facing the door, naked as a newborn, with only his Schofield in his hand.

Hank's voice boomed in the hallway. "Where is that son of a bitch?"

Women cried out in fear and doors slammed.

"Why's he coming for you?" Vanessa whispered.

"On account I insulted his tender ego yesterday," Owen replied, standing firm, his feet planted on the dusty wood floor.

"Is he in here?" Hank roared from the other side of the door.

"Are you gonna kill him?" Vanessa asked, shaking in fear.

"Yeah, I'm gonna kill him. Best look away if you don't want to see," Owen warned.

The door burst open, and in stepped Hank with a pistol in his grip. "There you—"

Owen didn't hesitate; he pulled the trigger then fanned the hammer two more times. All three rounds struck Hank center mass, sending him reeling back into the hallway, the wall stopping his backwards momentum.

Hank dropped his pistol, looking down at the holes in his shirt and the gathering blood that was soaking it. "You shot me."

"I didn't just shoot you, I've killed you," Owen said, walking towards him. He cocked the hammer again, leveled it at Hank's head and said, "You never come gunning for someone yelling and screaming. That was your first mistake. Your second was thinking you were tougher than you are." Owen squeezed the trigger, ending Hank's life.

Screams and wails of fear from the prostitutes filled the hallway.

Owen looked at the women and said, "Tell your boss I had no choice; he was coming for me. This was justified." He turned and went back into the room, slamming the door behind him.

Aroused by what she'd just witnessed, Vanessa leapt to her feet and rushed to Owen, wrapping her arms around him. "Are you sure we don't have time?"

"I'm afraid not. I need to be going and real quick," Owen said. He tossed on his clothes, grabbed his saddlebags, and rushed out the door. He stepped over Hank's body, now surrounded by a large pool of blood, and flew down the stairs and out of the bar without a word said to him. Not needing the attention from the law, he briskly walked to the livery and ran into the boy from yesterday.

"Hi, mister, you're late," the boy said.

"Something came up. I'll be needing my horse," Owen said, his eyes darting around looking for anyone coming towards him.

"Sure thing," the boy said, running off. Moments later he came back with the horse. "Mister, since you didn't pick him up before eight, it's another day's fee."

"Another day?" Owen protested.

"Sorry, but the boss—" the boy said before being interrupted.

"That's fine," Owen said, tossing the boy a couple of coins. He placed the saddlebags on the rear of the horse and helped the boy saddle him.

"You seem to be off in a rush, mister," the boy said.

"Like you said, I was late, so I'm a bit behind schedule," Owen replied.

With his horse ready, Owen walked him out and

looked around to find the streets looked normal. He mounted his horse and prodded him forward.

"See ya, mister," the boy said, waving.

Owen tipped his hat at the boy, faced forward and hollered, "Ya."

His horse responded by racing off at a full gallop, taking Owen down the street and out of town.

SHAPPAWAY COUNTY, OKLAHOMA TERRITORY

"Can we call it a day?" Grady said, slowing his horse to a walk.

Abigail looked back and hollered, "Another hour, let's get more miles under our belts."

"I'm whipped, woman, let's call it," Grady said, pulling the reins of his horse until it fully stopped.

Seeing he wasn't moving forward, Abigail turned Cloud around and trotted up to him. "Looks as if I was right about you."

"We did good today; that was eighty miles or so. That's respectable; it's not like we're in the cavalry. How about we give our horses a break for the day, make a fire and rest?" he said, leaning forward in the saddle to ease the pressure on his back.

Abigail rubbed Cloud's mane and looked around. The sun was just above the horizon to the west, and its rays cast long shadows across the tall grasses of the prairie. "I suppose you're right."

He sighed and yelled loudly, "Thank God." He dismounted and walked his horse to a flat spot. "This will work."

The two unsaddled their horses and secured their reins to a stake they hammered into the ground.

Abigail tied a feed bag over Cloud's head and patted her. "There you go, girl."

While she was tending to Cloud, Grady cleared out a spot for them to camp and gathered wood.

Their day had been long, but it was something Abigail was used to. She had often heard about the highlights of the journey, but no matter what, she always favored the destination more. If she could go faster, she would.

Grady spread out his bedroll and said, "I'm gonna sleep good tonight."

"Should we set up watch?" she asked.

He looked around and said, "We're in the middle of nowhere. There's not a soul out here but us."

"You're in the middle of nowhere with no one around until you're not," she said.

"Fine, but you have first watch. I'm eating then going to sleep right away," Grady complained.

The two worked together to set up the campsite for the night, with Abigail gathering more wood while Grady made a fire. When the sun finally set, the two sat on opposite sides of the fire, only the dancing flames separating them.

"This ride whooped you, didn't it?" she asked, a bit shocked by his demeanor. Gone was the charming Grady; now she had a chance to meet the grumpy one.

"I am tired. I can't believe you're not," he whined.

"I think my working with you is a better deal for you than me," she said.

"How so?" he asked.

"On account I think I'll toughen you up by the time we're done." She laughed.

He grunted something unintelligible, then asked, "Tell me, what exactly happened to Dwight, your last partner?"

"He was killed doing what he loved," she said.

"Was he gunned down in a gunfight, or was he shot in the back? How did it happen?" he asked, this time clarifying his question.

"It was an ambush; he saved my life," she replied.

"He did?"

"Yeah, some coward came at me with a double-barreled shotgun. Dwight saw it, shoved me out of the way, and took the blast. It killed him instantly," she said, her tone sounding subdued.

"I'm sorry to hear that," Grady said. "That was an honorable thing to do."

"He was an honorable man," she said.

"He must have cared for you deeply to sacrifice himself like that," Grady said.

"When I partner with someone, and I don't consider this a partnership by any stretch," she said, pointing between herself and Grady. "When I'm with a partner, we have each other's backs. We look out for the other. If I ever get a partner again, they'll have big boots to fill."

"They certainly will," Grady said, looking down and fiddling with a stick he held in his hand.

In the distance the howl of a coyote silenced their conversation.

"Did you know that coyotes never run alone, they're always in packs?"

"I'm aware," she said.

"I know Dwight was a good man, and you don't have to take my word, but I'm not too bad myself. I won't let you down, and I will cover your back if something happens," Grady said, knowing his words would never be enough for her.

"You said two things that are correct. First, Dwight was a good man, and second, I won't take your word for it. I'm the kind of person who needs someone to prove to me they are who they say they are," she said, taking a bite of dried meat.

Grady pulled out a flask and opened it.

"I don't care if you drink, but if you're going to with me around, don't get drunk. Remember, you have watch later," she said.

He put the flask to his lips but didn't take a sip. He grimaced, closed the lid, and pocketed the flask.

"I think it's best you get some shut-eye," she said, wrapping a blanket over her shoulders.

"Can you answer me a question?" he asked.

"Sure, but this is the last question for tonight," she said.

"How long do you think you'll do this for?"

Abigail thought about the question. She removed her hat and tossed it aside.

"Is that a hard question for you?" he asked.

"I'll do this for as long as I can," she replied.

He laughed.

"What's so funny?" she asked.

"Nothing, I just wasn't thinking that would be your answer. I would've thought it was something like 'until every outlaw has been captured.'"

"That's a foolish answer," she said.

"Why is that foolish?" he asked.

"Because there are too many outlaws to ever capture, and more are born each and every day. I do what I can do and will do so until such time presents itself that I'm incapable of doing it."

"That's a fair answer," he said, nodding.

"Now go to sleep. I don't want to hear you complaining tomorrow about how tired you are," she snapped.

"Yes, ma'am," he quipped as he stretched out along his bedroll. He pulled up a thick wool blanket enough to cover his chest and continued, "Say, what will you—"

"No more questions," she barked.

"They were right, mean as a viper," he shot back.

"If I'd known I'd be riding with a chatty woman, I would have said no. Now get some sleep. I'll wake you in a few hours," she said.

He rolled onto his side and closed his eyes. Within a minute he was fast asleep.

Abigail leaned back against her saddle and looked up into the vibrant sky, happy to finally have some peace. She began to trace out the constellations; it was a game she enjoyed playing. A memory came to her of when she'd taken Madeleine out to look at the night sky a few months back. It had started with her showing Madeleine how to find Ursa Major and ended with Madeleine telling her all about the planets Mars and Venus. She so enjoyed that night and longed for more like it in the future. As their evening came to a close, Abigail had shown her the North Star; overjoyed, Madeleine told Abigail that it would be their star. It would be the one thing always in the sky they could look to, and just maybe they'd be looking at it at the same time.

This memory brought a tear to Abigail's eye, which she quickly wiped away. She wasn't sure when she'd be back in Dallas to visit her, but prayed that day would come soon.

Grady began to snore loudly.

Abigail grunted her displeasure. She was tempted to wake him by tossing a rock but decided against it. She didn't know what to make of Grady just yet. He had his reputation, but who was the real man? What she'd come to know so far was a man who like to talk…a lot, a charmer and a seemingly polite individual; but who would he be when things went bad? This was the true test of anyone. How someone conducted themselves under pressure said everything, and soon she expected to find out; until then she'd keep her guard up and keep a watchful eye on him at all times.

CHAPTER THREE

HARTFORD RANCH, NOBLE COUNTY, OKLAHOMA TERRITORY

OCTOBER 9, 1893

When Allister heard the horse, he imagined it was Franklin returning early from his trip to town; then the distinct sound of a wagon's wheels hit his ears. He grabbed his shotgun, opened the front door, and stepped out to find Terrence Jones coming toward his house.

Terrence saw Allister emerge from the house with a shotgun and instantly regretted his decision to come over. He pulled the wagon close to the front and stopped. He engaged the brake and said, "Good morning, Allister."

"What the hell are you doing on my land, squatter?" Allister barked.

Terrence stiffened his spine and gulped at the sight of Allister standing tall with his double-barreled shotgun firmly in his hands. "I, um, I came to give you back your personal property."

"My what?" Allister asked.

"Is, um, is Franklin here?" Terrence asked, looking around the property, hoping Franklin was there, as he had a reputation of being the nicer brother.

"No, he's not. What the hell do you want?" Allister barked, his grip tightening around the forearm of the shotgun.

"Like I said, I came here out of courtesy to give you your personal property back. I found it on my land and—"

"You don't have any land, squatter!" Allister sneered.

"Now, Allister, I didn't come here to bicker or debate. I came out of courtesy, man to man, to tell you not to set up fencing on my land. I took the fence down—"

"You did what?" Allister said, raising the muzzle of the shotgun towards Terrence.

"Easy now, Allister, I came here in good faith. I don't want any trouble," Terrence said, his voice cracking with fear. His regret about coming was now turning into outright panic. *What on earth was I thinking?* he thought to himself.

"You took my fence down, and then you come over here spouting off about your land? Just who in the hell do you think you are, son?" Allister asked, the barrel hovering in the air and pointing directly at Terrence's chest. All he had to do was cock the hammers and pull the double triggers. Just that simple act would end this conversation and put an end to one of the men who had been causing him so much trouble.

"Like I said, I didn't come here to bicker. One of my cattle got stuck in the wire you set up. Now I'm willing to forgive that, but you can't be puttin' fence on my land."

"You said you didn't come here to bicker, but all I keep hearing is that. You come on my land after taking down my fence to tell me I'm on your land. Well, son, those are all lies, You're the squatter, and I don't give a damn what the government says. Those bastards can't be trusted, just ask those redskins if they can be trusted, just go ahead and ask them."

"I'm going to just drop off the fencing and wire here so you can use it for something else, but don't be setting it up—"

Once again, Allister interrupted Terrence. "Shut your mouth, squatter!" Allister advanced fast, placed the muzzle of the double barrels in Terrence's side, and barked, "If you say anything else about this being your land, I'll blow your guts all over the ground, do you hear me, boy?" Allister cocked the two hammers of the shotgun and jabbed it further into Terrence's side.

Terrence began to shake with fear. He had no idea what he had been thinking. This was a mistake of epic proportions, and if he didn't watch what he said, he'd be dead in a matter of seconds.

"Now get!" Allister hollered.

"Okay, I'm leaving," Terrence cried, taking the reins firmly in his hands and snapping, "Go, go." The horses jumped and began to canter off.

"If I see you on my land again, I'll kill you. Do you hear me? I'll put an end to your life, you damn squatter!" Allister hollered.

Terrence snapped the reins repeatedly on his horses until they were running at a gallop.

Allister stood his ground and watched Terrence ride out of sight. "The nerve of that son of a bitch. How dare he come on my land!" Allister screamed. The more he thought about it, the greater his anger welled up inside.

The mere audacity of Terrence being there showed a level of disrespect he hadn't experienced since he was a young man living under his father's roof. He thought the squatters must feel empowered to act because nothing had happened to them.

Unable to control his anger, Allister raced to the barn, saddled his horse, and took off after Terrence. He wasn't going to be disrespected, nope, not on his land. Riding as fast and as hard as he could, Allister caught up with Terrence only because he had slowed down once he felt he was a safe distance. Coming up alongside, Allister leveled the barrels of the shotgun and hollered, "You think you can come onto my land and talk that way, squatter!"

Terrence whipped the team of horses but couldn't pull away fast enough.

Allister pulled both triggers, unleashing two barrels of double-aught buckshot. The shot struck Terrence on the right flank, neck and face. The blast was strong enough that he fell from the wagon and tumbled onto the hard ground. He scrambled to get to his feet, but not before Allister leapt from his horse and thrust an eight-inch blade into his back.

Terrence wailed in pain, his arms flailing as he tried to remove the knife that stuck out of the center of his back, in between his shoulder blades.

Allister kicked him to the ground, placed his left foot squarely on his back, and pulled out the blade. "You sons of bitches think you can just show up and take what is mine. I'm not having any of it. How dare you!"

"Please, no, don't. I have a wife and a child," Terrence pleaded as blood poured from his mouth.

"Know where I'm going next? I'm riding to that shack you call a house and I'm going to kill that whore of a wife and that runt you call a boy!" Allister screamed, spit flying from his mouth as he spoke.

"Please, no, I'll leave, I'll go. Just don't kill me, please!" Terrence cried out.

Powerless to control his temper, Allister howled in anger, "It's too late for that!" He ripped his Remington Model 1890 revolver from a holster on his hip, cocked it, aimed the sights at the back of Terrence's head, and pulled the trigger. The .44-40-caliber round smashed into Terrence's head and exited through his face. It was all that was needed to end his life.

With Terrence dead, Allister holstered his Remington and stared at the body on the ground. Killing him hadn't satiated his anger. He couldn't just kill the man, he needed to send a clear message once and for all that he meant business, and those whom he considered squatters had two choices, leave or meet the same fate as Terrence.

He loaded Terrence's body onto his wagon, tied his own horse to the back, and rode the wagon back to his house. There he'd formulate a plan for what to do next.

POTTAWATOMIE COUNTY, OKLAHOMA TERRITORY

Abigail and Grady woke early and set out. By midday they had ridden thirty miles and were set to repeat what they'd done the day before.

Grady wasn't as talkative today, mostly due to being tired, and for that Abigail was thankful.

As they were close to cresting a gradual slope, they heard the crack of a gunshot. Both brought their horses to a stop and listened.

A second gunshot was followed by the scream of a woman.

Following her instincts, Abigail ripped her Winchester from the scabbard and raced up the slope.

"Where are you going?" Grady asked.

Abigail ignored Grady. If someone was in trouble, she was there to help. It was part of her code. She dismounted Cloud just shy of the top of the slope. She low crawled the remaining distance until she could get a good vantage point of the area beneath her.

There she saw a covered wagon. The horses that had been pulling the wagon were lying down, no doubt dead. Surrounding the wagon were debris and personal effects.

Two men on horses with rifles in their hands rode up and dismounted.

Abigail could hear they were talking but couldn't make out what they were saying.

Grady came up behind her and said, "What the hell are you doing?"

"It sounds as if someone's in trouble," she replied, looking through her binoculars.

"This ain't our business. Let's just move around them and keep heading to Perry," he said.

She gave him a cross look and said, "If you don't

want to help, then move on."

He grunted his disapproval but remained.

Through the binoculars, she saw the two men move closer to the wagon; then screams came.

Abigail couldn't see who was screaming, but it sounded like a woman, and these men were clearly not relations to her. Having seen enough, Abigail dropped the binoculars and picked up her rifle.

"Are you really gonna shoot those men?" Grady asked, shocked by her determination to inject herself into the situation.

She raised the rear sight aperture and adjusted it for the distance. Once she was set, she got behind the rifle and took aim on the first man that came into view.

"Answer me," Grady said.

"Shut your mouth. I'm trying to focus," Abigail said, placing the sights on the man's back. She exhaled, placed her index finger on the trigger, and began to apply steady and even pressure.

The man reached the wagon, eliciting more screams from inside it.

Abigail kept applying pressure on the trigger until it fired. The round struck the man squarely in the chest. He dropped to the ground dead. She cycled the lever-action rifle, realigned herself, found the other man and took aim. Moments later, her second shot exploded out of the barrel and traveled the two hundred and ten yards to its final destination, the second man's chest. It struck him just above the heart and sent him reeling backwards. He fell to the ground, twitching for a few seconds before becoming still.

"We're done here," she said, hopping to her feet and whistling loudly.

Cloud trotted up.

She leapt onto his back and took off towards the wagon, leaving Grady looking on in awe. She covered the distance quickly, arriving to find more than just the two men she'd shot, but another man and a teenaged boy, who had also been shot. "My name is Abigail. I'm here to help," she called out to whoever was in the wagon.

"Please hurry," a woman cried.

Abigail jumped off Cloud and ran up to the back of the wagon. She peered in to find a woman, her shirt covered in blood, holding a young boy, who appeared either dead or unconscious. "Ma'am, how can I help?"

"It's Charles, he's been shot," the woman said.

Abigail climbed into the back of the wagon and examined the boy, only to find he was dead. "Ma'am, I'm so sorry, but your son—"

"NO!" she wailed.

Angered, she sat back and looked on as the woman cried.

Grady appeared suddenly, startling the woman.

"Get back!" the woman screamed.

"Ma'am, it's fine. He's with me," Abigail explained.

Wild-eyed, the woman stared at Abigail and asked, "Why? Why would people do this? Why?"

"Some people are just evil, ma'am," Abigail replied.

"Abby, what can I do to help?" Grady asked.

"Let me find out," Abigail said, turning to the

woman. "Ma'am, we're here for you. Tell us what we can do."

The woman looked at Abigail for a second, then fainted.

Abigail went to her side, picked up her head, and placed it in her lap. It was then she noticed the woman wasn't just covered in her son's blood but her own; she too had been shot. "Grady, she's got a round in her gut. She's bleeding out."

The woman came to and stared at Abigail. "Why?"

"Ma'am, you've been shot too. I need to tend to your wound. Okay?" Abigail said then reached down to unbutton her dress to get a better idea of the wound.

"No, stop," the woman said, grabbing Abigail's hand.

"But, ma'am, I need to see how bad it is," Abigail said.

"No, I don't want to be helped. I want to stay right here with my family," she said.

Abigail looked at the woman then gave Grady a look of despair.

Grady shrugged his shoulders and walked away.

"Ma'am, you've been shot. I need to tend to the wound. So please let me see," Abigail said.

The woman shook her head.

"I can't help you if you won't let me," Abigail said.

"If you want to help me," the woman said, taking Abigail's hand and guiding it back to the back strap of her Colt, "then you know what to do."

"I can't do that," Abigail said.

"Then leave, go," the woman said, pushing Abigail

away and reaching for her son's body.

"Ma'am, please let me help you," Abigail said.

"If you're not willing to do that, then go," the woman said, her voice growing weak from the blood loss.

"Don't you want to live?" Abigail asked.

"What's there to live for?" the woman countered.

Abigail looked at her, then to the boy, then outside to the two bodies of her husband and her other son.

"They were my life and now it's gone. You might be able to fix me up, but I have nothing now," she said, grimacing from the pain in her lower abdomen.

Abigail hadn't ever been in this sort of situation before. For the first time in her life, she was treading unfamiliar waters.

"Oh, my baby boy," the woman cried, caressing the boy's bloody cheek.

Tears welled up in Abigail's eyes as she imagined the boy was Madeleine and she was the woman. What would she want?

Outside, she could hear Grady digging. He was one step ahead of her.

"My precious, precious boy," the woman sobbed.

Abigail removed her Colt with a trembling hand and looked at it.

The woman gave her a glance and nodded; she had accepted her fate. She reached and gently took Abigail's hand and brought the muzzle of the barrel to her temple. She again gave Abigail a glance and nodded.

More tears streamed down Abigail's cheeks. She grasped the woman's hand with her left and put her right index finger on the trigger. "Forgive me."

"No, my dear, thank you," the woman said and closed her eyes.

Abigail closed hers too and pulled the trigger.

The sound of the shot brought Grady back to the wagon. He looked in and saw Abigail holding the pistol, smoke coming from the barrel. He knew what she'd done, and was fine with it. "I'll go back to digging the graves."

Abigail remained in the wagon until Grady returned hours later.

"I have the graves dug," he said.

Abigail wiped the tears from her cheeks and helped him take the bodies from the wagon. Gently, the two laid them into the shallow graves and covered them.

Out of sorts, Abigail allowed Grady to say a prayer. She couldn't get what had just happened out of her head. She'd seen so much death before, had killed more than a few in her days; but today had really jolted her. Was it because she saw a bit of herself in the woman?

Never one to pass up on valuables, Grady gathered all he could find and strapped it to their two new horses.

Abigail didn't say a word, nor did she help; she just stared off.

When he was done, he asked, "Abby, are you okay?"

She looked deeply into his eyes and said, "No, I'm not. This really affected me; I can't explain why."

"Sometimes you never know what will do it, but know that it's okay. I've had my days too."

"Thank you for burying them without complaint."

"Of course, it was the right thing to do," he said. "And I want to apologize about what I said on the hill."

"It's fine. I've just never been one to sit around and let evil men do their deeds."

"I see that now."

"C'mon, let's ride. We have another forty miles ahead of us today," she said, taking Cloud by the reins.

"We can take a break if you want."

She looked at the freshly dug graves and said, "No, let's get riding. The quicker I get away from this, the better I'll feel."

HARTFORD RANCH, NOBLE COUNTY, OKLAHOMA TERRITORY

"Damn it, Allister, what have you done?" Franklin cried out upon seeing Terrence's body lying out in front of his house.

"Why are you bitching? We're planning on having them all killed anyway," Allister replied.

"But we're having someone else do it. We can't have the blood on our hands," Franklin said.

"What's the damn difference, huh? It's all the same to the law. Do you somehow think it's legal to kill as long as you hire someone to do it for ya? And I thought you were the smart one," Allister barked.

"This is not the plan," Franklin wailed.

"It is what it is, brother. Now help me figure out how we're going to handle his body," Allister said.

"Bury it," Franklin replied.

"No, how do we use it to send the others a message?" Allister said.

Franklin began to pace back and forth. Each time he passed the body, he looked down at it and grunted. "Damn it, damn it, damn it."

"Calm down, little brother; we've done worse," Allister said, reminding him of their past.

"We came to Oklahoma to start new, to become legitimate. Not become murderers."

"Well, it's done now. I think I should wrap his body in the wire and drop it off at Oscar's house. That pesky son of a bitch needs to know we're serious," Allister said.

"No!" Franklin snapped.

"Why not?" Allister asked, shrugging his shoulders.

"Because that could spiral out of control. We don't know if the US Marshal might come snooping around. We can't risk it," Franklin said.

"The US Marshal? That idiot isn't even within three hundred miles of here. Nor does he care," Allister said.

"Al, you're right, what's done is done; but let's just bury the body and go back to the plan."

Now Allister began to pace back and forth. The temptation to taunt Oscar and the others was appealing to him, but as a practical man, he understood what Franklin was saying.

"Please, let's just bury the body, burn the wagon—"

"No, I'm keeping the wagon. That's a perfectly fine wagon," Allister said. "Consider it payment for tearing down my fence."

"Fine, but can we please bury the body?" Franklin

asked.

Allister removed his pipe bag from his pocket. He packed the bowl and thought about what Franklin proposed.

"Well?"

"You want to bury him so bad, you do it," Allister said, sticking the pipe between his teeth.

"I didn't kill him," Franklin protested.

"But I don't want to bury him," Allister countered.

Franklin paused for a second then began to chuckle. "We sound like quarreling brothers, don't we?"

"We do, 'cause we are," Allister said.

"I'll bury him, but no more killing these squatters. We stick to the plan. Have the hired guns do all the dirty work swiftly so nothing gets out. Okay?"

Allister shrugged his shoulders, turned and said, "Don't bury him near the house. I don't want his rotting corpse stinking up the place."

***

Franklin smoothed out the dark rich dirt and tossed the shovel aside. Sweat streaked down his face, and his shirt was drenched. He couldn't recall the last time he'd buried someone, and even if he did, he didn't remember it being so much work.

He put the tools in the barn and headed to the house. The sun had set and he could smell something cooking.

Before entering the house, he stopped by a trough

filled with water and washed the dirt and sweat from his arms and face. The entire time he'd been burying Terrence, he fretted over the consequences of the killing. He knew soon people would come looking for him, and no doubt that search would most likely lead to their homestead. *What was Allister thinking?* he thought.

Allister had always had a short fuse, making him quick to anger, and when he went there, violence soon followed. After having to deal with so many years of violence under his roof as a child, then living it while he rode with Allister's gang, he had been happy to hear about the opportunity in Oklahoma and had looked forward to settling down, free to live a life free of violence. Then like always, Allister found conflict; this time because he didn't do his due diligence. Now they found themselves in a fight for the land they'd been on for months, but Franklin now had a backup plan, and that was his lots in town. If somehow they lost the rights to this land, he'd build a saloon and move in above it. What would happen to Allister? Well, that would have to be determined; he just prayed that Allister's signature anger didn't spell doom for that too.

He toweled himself off and entered the house to find Allister stirring a cauldron that hung over the flames in the fireplace. "Smells good."

"It's beef stew," Allister said.

"I'm starving," Franklin said, pulling a chair from the table and sitting down.

"Is Terry taken care of proper like?" Allister asked, his attention still focused on the stew.

"Yes, I buried him fifty feet south of the barn. He's well out of sight of anyone who happens to come visit," Franklin replied.

Allister turned and said, "If anyone comes to visit, they'll find a spot next to the bastard."

"Let's stop doing our own killing and leave it up to the professionals," Franklin said.

"Where are they anyway?" Allister asked. "You said that Blake feller would be here by now."

"I don't know. Maybe he'll arrive tomorrow," Franklin said, leaning back in the chair and stretching his weary muscles. Thoughts came of his lots in town and how he couldn't wait to get to work on the saloon. He knew Allister would find out; he just wanted the building up so he could show something to his brother when that time came.

"As soon as he gets here, put him to work. I'm tired of waiting," Allister said.

"I can tell," Franklin joked.

"I'll admit, I quite enjoyed killing that bastard. Serves him right, thinking he could come onto my land and talk to me the way he did," Allister sneered.

"I understand, brother, but no more. When these gunmen come, let's put them to work. That'll free us up to get the ranch up and running," Franklin said.

A knock at the door startled the brothers.

Allister tossed the large metal spoon, grabbed his shotgun, and cocked the hammers. "If it's one of those squatters, they'll be joining old Terry in the field."

Franklin jumped up and ran to a coat peg near the

door. There he had his gun belt hanging. He removed his Colt, cocked it and called out, "Who is it?"

"It's Owen Blake. I'm looking for a Franklin Hartford."

Franklin's eyes widened. He gave Allister a quick glance and whispered loudly, "It's him, he's here."

"Well, open the damn door and let the man in," Allister said, uncocking the hammers on the shotgun and putting it back above the mantel.

Franklin uncocked his Colt and slipped it back in his holster. He opened the latch on the door and opened it wide to see the hulking Owen standing tall in his black outfit. Around his waist hung his silver-studded gun belt and holsters. "Evening, Mr. Blake."

"You Mr. Hartford?" Owen asked.

"Yes, sir, I am. Come on in, please," Franklin said, stepping aside and giving Owen a wide berth.

Owen looked at Franklin then gave Allister a cautious gaze. "Mind if I grab my saddlebags and put my horse in your barn first?"

"Of course," Franklin replied. "Let me help you." Franklin scurried out and waved for Owen to follow him.

Owen did just that, taking the horse to the barn and removing the saddle and saddlebags. "Something smelled good up there."

"My brother has a beef stew on. I guarantee it's going to be great, real stick-to-your-ribs food. I bet you're hungry after your ride today."

"I am," Owen said, tossing the saddlebags over his shoulder.

"Then follow me to the house. We'll get you fed and discuss the job at hand," Franklin said. As they walked, Franklin noticed Owen carried two Smith and Wesson Schofield revolvers. "You're a Smith and Wesson man, huh?"

"Huh?" Owen asked.

"Your sidearms—I'm a Colt man," Franklin said as he weakly attempted to make conversation.

"Yeah, I like the Smiths," Owen said.

"Is it true that the cylinder ejector fails sometimes?" Franklin asked, referring to the proprietary ejector system that Smith and Wesson had in the cylinder. The Smith and Wesson design was unique, enabling the operator to use a top break on the pistol to open it up and eject all the cases simultaneously. This design also made it easier to reload.

"I've never had an issue," Owen replied.

"Do you use it because of your time in the army?" Franklin asked.

Owen stopped and said, "Stop asking me questions. I'm finding it annoying."

"I've got just one more. Can you tell me why you answered my advertisement for the job?"

"On account I heard it paid well," Owen replied honestly.

"It does, one hundred per head," Franklin said, smiling pridefully. Getting to the house, he opened the door for Owen. "Come on in and get settled.

Owen lowered his head slightly to allow clearance for his towering frame and entered the house. "Where can I put these?" he asked, nodding to his saddlebags.

Like a doting mother, Franklin went to take the saddlebags, but Owen rebuffed him. "I'll handle my own things."

"Of course, my apologies," Franklin said. "You can put them over in that corner near that cot; in fact, that's where you can sleep tonight. That's normally where I lay my head, but you can take it while you're here."

Allister stood quietly in the corner of the room, watching Owen's subtle movements.

Owen sauntered over and tossed the bags on the cot. "I'm hungry."

"We've got stew," Franklin said, rushing to the cauldron. He scooped a large portion into a bowl and placed it on the table. "Want some bread with that?"

"Sure," Owen said, taking a seat. He lowered his head over the stew and inhaled. "Smells good."

Franklin returned with bread on a plate and set it next to Owen.

Not wanting to wait to eat himself, Allister scooped a bowl and took a seat opposite Owen.

Owen dove into the stew, filling his mouth with a large spoonful.

Franklin hovered near the table.

"You're making me nervous. Sit down and eat with me," Owen said to Franklin.

"Yes, of course," Franklin said and rushed to make himself a bowl.

Allister found Franklin's behavior peculiar. He didn't know what to make of it.

Franklin joined them at the table and immediately began to eat. Curious about Owen's travels, Franklin asked with his mouth full, "What were you doing in Kansas?"

"Work," Owen simply answered.

"What specifically?" Franklin asked.

"Frank, give the man a break with the questions. He just arrived; he's tired and hungry. Let him eat in peace," Allister barked.

"I'm merely trying to make polite conversation," Franklin fired back.

Taking the bread, Owen tore off a piece and soaked it in the stew. "How many are you needing killed?"

Franklin gulped. "I never said we needed them killed, specifically, just gotten rid of."

Owen cracked a smile and said, "That means killed. Listen, if I was brought in, you need people killed not herded up."

"A decent number," Allister replied.

"How many?" Owen asked again.

Franklin knew the number exactly and blurted it out. "Fourteen."

"Does that include Terry?" Allister asked.

"Sorry, thirteen," Franklin replied.

"So thirteen hundred dollars to kill these squatters for ya? Is there anything I should know minus the specifics like where I can find them and those other details?" Owen asked.

Allister furrowed his brow. "You're mistaken; it's not thirteen hundred. It would be less. We're only paying fifty per head for the children."

Owen stopped chewing his food and gave Allister a hard stare. "You want me to kill children?"

"Yes," Allister replied bluntly.

"You're not being funny with me? You want me to kill children and are only willing to pay half?" Owen asked, now placing his gaze on Franklin.

"We, um, my brother feels that if we don't…you see, I told him about how the Romans—" Franklin said before being interrupted.

"I don't give a damn about killing children. What I don't understand is you want to pay half. A killing is a killing; there's no discount," Owen clarified.

"But they're easy, they don't fight back. I figured I was—" Allister said before he too was stopped short.

"Killing is killing, period. If you want this issue solved and you want me to kill children, then you pay the same," Owen said plainly.

"Fair enough, a hundred per head," Allister said. He felt a tinge of apprehension about Owen. It was an uncommon feeling for him, but there was something very dark about him.

"Now have you called for other hired guns to come?" Owen asked.

"Yes," Franklin answered.

"You don't need them. I can handle it all," Owen declared then shoveled a spoonful of stew into his mouth.

"I've got four others coming. They'll be arriving soon," Franklin said.

"You don't need them. I've got this covered all by

myself," Owen said.

"You're one man. If we're going to do this right, we need all five," Allister said.

"When are they expected to arrive?" Owen asked, putting his spoon down.

Allister straightened his spine and answered, "Frank says tomorrow probably."

"I work alone, but I'll overlook that as long as the others do as I say," Owen said, getting up from the table and marching over to the cot and sitting down.

Franklin leaned in towards Allister and whispered, "Don't upset him."

"Fine, but if this causes a problem with the others, you're paying for it out of your share," Allister said and returned to eating.

"I'll take care of everything." Franklin craned his head back and said, "Mr. Blake, I'll talk to the others when they arrive. I'll make sure they know, but I can't necessarily control them."

"Good, now tell me the specifics. Where can I find these squatters and so forth?" Owen asked, removing his boots.

Franklin spent the next thirty minutes detailing everything Owen would need to know, from where each one lived to the exact number per family.

Owen didn't take notes; he merely nodded and asked any questions if he needed more information for the job. When he had what he needed, Owen smiled and said, "I like eggs, two with bacon."

"Huh?" Allister asked from the table, where he sat

packing his pipe.

"For my breakfast. I'll need a good meal before I head out, and you should know I like to start early," Owen said, stretching out on the cot.

Allister sneered at Franklin. If there was one thing he hated, it was being ordered around in his own house. However, he quickly let it go. If Owen was the man Franklin said he was, and could easily handle their issues with Oscar and the others, then he'd suffer through these slight indignities.

CHAPTER FOUR

MILKE HOMESTEAD, NOBLE COUNTY, OKLAHOMA TERRITORY

OCTOBER 10, 1893

"Oscar, come out here!" Agatha cried from outside the house.

Sticking his head out the door, Oscar was greeted by the early morning sun. The warm rays felt good on his face. "What do you need?" he hollered.

"It's Pamela Jones. She's here about Terrence," Agatha said. "She wants to know if we've seen him."

Oscar emerged from the house, wiping his hands on a clean cloth. He'd just been trimming some meat he'd taken from a hog he'd slaughtered. "What's this about Terry?"

"Have you seen him?" Pamela asked, a look of panic in her eyes.

"No, I haven't seen him since the other day in town," Oscar replied.

"He said he had somewhere to go and left in the wagon. That was yesterday late morning," Pamela said.

"Why don't you come inside. I'll make you some tea," Agatha said, walking up alongside Pamela, who was atop a horse.

"I can't be long. I've left Thaddeus in charge of his younger brother at home. I just need to know if you know where he might be," Pamela said, her voice showing signs of strain. Thaddeus was nine years old, and his two younger brother, Jackson was four.

"I'm sorry, Pamela, I don't know where he might be. Did he give an indication at all about where he might be going?" Oscar asked.

"None, he left in the wagon and just told me he had somewhere to go. Nothing, well, maybe something, but I know he wouldn't," she replied.

Clueing in on her comment, Oscar asked, "Wouldn't what?"

"He was going on about going out to Franklin and Allister's house. He found they had put up some wire fencing. Terry took it down and told me he was going to take it to them. Said something about declaring they stay off our land. I told him not to be a damn fool; he calmed down and said nothing more about it. Lord, I hope he didn't go over there."

"I'm sure he didn't," Agatha said, giving Oscar a peculiar look.

"Who else have you talked to?" Oscar asked.

"You're the first; I'm heading over to see the McGreeleys next," she said, referring to Robert and his wife, Candace.

"Pam, how about you head home? I'll go ride out to see everyone then head into town for you, ask around see if anyone has seen him," Oscar said.

"That's a good idea, Pamela. Let Oscar do that. Go back to your boys," Agatha said, taking Pamela's hand. She felt for her friend and knew how stressful it must be not knowing where Terrence was.

"Are you sure? I don't want to put you out," Pamela said.

"I'm sure Agatha can finish carving up the pig," Oscar said, giving Agatha a nod.

"It's fine. Let us help you, Pamela. This is what good neighbors do for each other," Agatha said.

"Thank you both, and please, if you find him, tell him to come home right away. His family is deeply concerned for him," Pamela said.

"I'll tell him," Oscar said.

"God bless you both," Pamela said, turning her horse around and trotting off.

When Pamela was out of earshot, Agatha turned to Oscar and asked, "What do you make of this?"

"I've got some concerns, but I just don't think he'd do it," Oscar said, giving a clue he knew where Terrence might be.

"What does that mean?" she asked, crossing her arms and giving him a quizzical look.

"It means I might know where he went," Oscar confessed.

"And why didn't you tell the poor woman? You can see she's worried sick," Agatha chastised.

"On account I don't want to give anyone undo worry until I can confirm it," Oscar replied.

"Where do you think he is?" Agatha pressed.

"I saw him in town the other day. He got talking about how he'd found some fencing. Said he was going over to see Allister, give him an earful. He mentioned that

Pamela talked him down."

"But you think he might have gone?" Agatha asked, her arms crossed with her fingers nervously tapping.

"I might have talked him into it."

"Lord, God in heaven, please tell me you didn't do that. Please, Oscar, tell me you didn't send that man to his grave by getting all uppity and filling him with dreams of fighting back," Agatha snapped.

"I did," Oscar replied, his head hung low out of shame.

"Oscar Milke, you know those men are dangerous. Why on earth would you talk him into going over there?" she asked.

"I'm so fed up with those brothers. We can't sit around and let them think they have the rights to this land. This is ours," Oscar declared.

Agatha approached Oscar and said, "I agree with you, but you can't be doing or saying anything half-cocked. How are you going to find out if he went over there?"

"I'll go over there myself and see," Oscar said, although deep down he was fearful of the idea.

"No you won't, you can't. If Terry went there and something horrible happened, I'm not having you suffer the same fate," she said.

"Then what do I tell Pamela?" Oscar asked.

"You tell her the truth; then you get Robert to ride over with you," she blared.

"I'll do this, I'll go into town first, see if he's there. Maybe he just decided to let the bottle get the better of him," Oscar said.

"You know he's not a drinker," Agatha said.

"At least let me see if he's there or if someone has seen him before I get Robert and ride out to see the brothers. Best I turn over all stones first, 'cause the second we ride up on them, it's certain to escalate," Oscar said.

"Can't we get the marshal to do anything?" she asked.

"I've said this many times, he's gone; there's no law in these parts. These matters need to be handled by us for now," he said, giving her a nod and heading towards the barn to get his horse.

"You be careful, you hear me, and no riding over to their house unless you have Robert with you. I can't afford to lose you; you hear me, Oscar?"

"Understood," Oscar replied, waving his hand.

NOBLE COUNTY, OKLAHOMA TERRITORY

Abigail couldn't shake the achy feeling that she felt across her body, and sweat was pouring off her face. She could feel the fever but didn't want to admit even to herself that she was ill. She had woken that morning feeling a bit out of sorts and just thought it was lack of sleep after a hard day's ride. However, it was now late morning and the feeling was only getting worse, so much that Grady took notice.

"Are you doing okay?" he asked.

"I'm fine," she said, brushing off his comment. One

thing she was never good at was being honest when it came to her health and well-being; mainly she didn't want to seem weak and in need.

"You don't look that good; in fact, you look God-awful," he said slowing down and trotting next to her. "We can stop and rest for a bit, it's okay."

"I'm fine. If anything is bothering me, it's you running your mouth all the time," she growled.

"Damn it, Abby, stop being so darn ornery. You don't look good. You're covered in sweat, and your face is pasty white," he growled back.

"Please stop talking. Your voice sounds like someone is stabbing my ears," she countered, her head bowed down low.

He trotted just ahead of her, forcing Cloud to stop.

"What are you doing?" she asked.

He dismounted and went to her side. "Get off the horse and rest. We're almost there. We can afford a short break."

Deciding not to argue, she went to get off Cloud but found her body overcome with fatigue. Almost toppling to the hard ground, Grady took her by the arms and helped her down. "Get my bedroll," she said.

Grady slid the bedroll from behind her saddle and unfolded it on the ground a few feet away. "Come, lie down."

She stumbled his way and plopped down on the ground. "This might be a good idea. I am feeling a bit under the weather."

He removed her hat; it was soaked with sweat.

Touching her forehead with the back side of his hand, he said, "You've got a fever. You're burning up."

"My eyes feel like they're on fire," she mumbled.

"I'm going to just look at the top of your chest, make sure you don't have a rash or anything; just know I'm not getting fresh with you," Grady warned.

Abigail nodded.

He unbuttoned the top few buttons of her drenched shirt and examined her skin but found nothing but glistening sweat. "You look fine." His concern was smallpox, and fortunately she didn't have any rashes or lesions…yet. He went and got some water and brought it back. "Here, take a sip," he said, putting the canteen to her lips.

She slowly sipped.

"Darn it, Abby, why didn't you tell me you weren't feeling well?" Grady asked, frustrated with her.

"You go ahead. Find your contact in town," she said.

"I'm not leaving you. We'll stay put right here. That job can wait," he said.

"No, please go," she urged.

"Not going to happen. I'm gonna take care of you," he said, getting up and going to his horse.

"Why?"

He stopped and said, "'Cause you'd do the same for me."

***

Oscar raced to town and asked anyone who might know,

but no one had seen Terrence. Each time he received a no, his fears worsened that his friend had taken his ill advice and gone out to confront the Hartford brothers.

After exhausting every lead in town, he made his way towards Robert's house, which was closest to town. As he rode, he recited to himself just how he'd explain the situation and prayed that Robert would join him on going out to the Hartford's to see about Terrence. He knew it would be a tough sell, but it had to be done, and it did feel like a tremendous amount of responsibility.

In the distance he saw four horses standing with no apparent riders. Curious, he made his way to them to investigate. The closer he got, the more nervous he became. He placed his right hand on the back strap of his pistol and slowed down his horse to a canter.

A head popped up and looked at Oscar. It was Grady and he had his rifle firmly in his shoulder. "Just hold up there."

Hearing Grady's warning, Oscar did as he asked and came to a full stop. "I saw the horses. Wasn't sure if they had gotten out of their stables."

Abigail mumbled something unintelligible.

Grady gave her a glance. She was getting worse by the minute. "You live close by?"

"About a half hour away," Oscar replied.

"My partner here needs some help," Grady said.

"What's wrong with her?" Oscar asked.

"She's taken ill. I need a place, a home or something, where she can rest up. How far is Perry?" Grady asked.

Having been raised by a pastor, Oscar knew the

importance of providing shelter to those in need, yet his travels had calloused his generosity and hardened him to the world. "Perry is about seven miles north."

Grady lowered his rifle and grunted his displeasure at Oscar's reply.

"I might know another place," Oscar said.

"You do?" Grady asked. He desperately wanted to get her somewhere proper to rest while he went to meet up with his employers.

"It's my place. It's just a couple of miles that way," Oscar said, pointing west.

"We can stay in a barn. Anything will do," Grady said.

"She doesn't have the pox, does she?" Oscar asked, suddenly becoming worried about whom he might be taking with him to his place.

"No, sir, she's got a fever and is weak; she just needs a safe place to rest while I go conduct some business," Grady said.

"Mind if I ride up?" Oscar asked.

Grady motioned him over.

Oscar rode up and looked down on Abigail. "Your partner is a woman?"

"Does that matter?" Grady asked.

"I, um, I assumed your partner would be a man. Is she your wife?"

"No, she's not," Grady answered.

"I have a shed you can put her in," Oscar said.

"Thank you," Grady said.

"Where you two heading?" Oscar asked,

dismounting his horse.

"To Perry, we have some business to conduct," Grady replied.

Curious, Oscar continued to question Grady. "What sort of business brings you to Perry?"

Not wanting to tell a man he didn't know specifically what they were doing there, he lied and said, "Prospecting."

"Prospecting? For what?" Oscar asked, shocked to hear a prospector would be in the area.

"Ore, iron ore," Grady said, again lying.

"Hmm," Oscar mused, rubbing his chin and thinking.

To Grady, the lie appeared to be working, as Oscar's expression was one of surprise not disbelief.

"You just never know what you can earn a dollar for in Oklahoma, do you?" Oscar asked, smiling.

"Say, care to help me get her on my horse?" Grady asked.

"Sure thing," Oscar replied.

With Oscar's help, the two got Abigail in the saddle of Grady's horse.

"Abby, can you hold on?" Grady asked.

She nodded.

"I didn't catch your name," Oscar said, mounting his horse.

"Grady, my name is Grady. And my partner, her name is Abigail," Grady answered. It was the one truth he was willing to part with today.

"Nice to meet you. My name is Oscar Milke."

"How far did you say?" Grady asked.

"It's close by," Oscar replied, again pointing west.

Grady mounted his horse; sitting just behind Abby, he placed his arms around her and took the reins. "I've got a safe place so you can rest. I just need you to be patient."

Abigail mumbled again.

Oscar turned his horse and started towards his house with Grady and Abigail following.

At the moment, all Grady could think about was Abigail's health. It was ironic that he'd wanted her to join him on this job so he could leverage her expertise; but now he was having to help her. He didn't know what was wrong with her but prayed it wasn't the beginning of a severe ailment.

***

Owen set out early to reconnoiter all the homesteads of the families. Using a pocket-sized booklet, he sketched out how each lay and plotted the distances between them; this way he'd be able to draw up a final plan that he'd execute as soon as possible.

He climbed a small rise and found himself not twenty feet from two riders. Both looked like capable men with sidearms and rifles in scabbards.

"Whoa," one of the men said, pulling back on the reins of his horse before placing one hand on the back strap of his pistol. "Howdy, mister."

Owen stopped his horse and sized them up quickly.

The second man, who was slender with a long torso, smiled and leaned his weight on the horn of his saddle. "Good day to ya. Could you point me and my friend in the direction of Perry?"

Owen cleared his throat. He kept his eyes on the first man, who still had the palm of his hand on his pistol. "It's northeast of here, maybe seven miles or so," Owen said, nodding in the direction he was suggesting they go.

The second man removed his hat and, using his sleeve, wiped his brow. "It's a warm day, isn't it."

"I suppose it might be warm for some," Owen replied, his eyes still fixed on the first man.

Noting Owen's hard stare, the second man reached out to his partner and said, "Ease up, Joe."

Joe, who appeared younger than the second man, did as he was told. "If you say so, Earl."

"Say, are you a local?" Earl asked Owen.

"You have a lot of questions," Owen said, switching his stare to Earl.

"I'm just being friendly. I don't mean anything by it," Earl replied.

Owen remembered that other bounty hunters were coming into town, and these men fit that description.

"Are you two here to meet with a Mr. Hartford?" Owen asked.

Both Earl and Joe raised their brows, shocked by the direct question. Joe gave Earl a nervous glance and said, "Who's asking?"

"I think you just answered my question," Owen said. "If you're here to see them, I can take you direct."

"You can?" Earl said.

Owen spit out tobacco juice, wiped the dribble from his chin, and replied, "I can."

"Are you Mr. Hartford?" Joe asked.

"Joe, he ain't Mr. Hartford. If I were to guess, this gentleman here is a bounty hunter like us," Earl said, shifting in his saddle.

"My name is Owen Blake."

Earl's face grew ashen. "You're the Butcher of Bloody Creek."

"I am," Owen replied proudly.

"Did you really have all those Indians slaughtered? Is that true?" Earl asked, stiffening his back to appear larger in the saddle.

"Every man, woman and child," Owen confessed.

Joe crowed in surprise at Owen's admission. "You're a bloodthirsty killer."

Owen squinted and gave a throaty laugh. "If I'm anything, I'm a killer. It's as though God gave me the talent."

"Or the devil," Earl said, interrupting Owen.

Owen cocked his head and placed his gaze squarely on Earl, who he now knew was the older and more experienced gunfighter.

The tension rose quickly between them.

Joe eased his hand back towards his pistol again but was clumsy doing it.

Seeing the move, Owen drew his Schofield, cocked it, and shot Earl.

The bullet smashed into Earl's chest and exploded

out his back.

Owen pivoted and aimed the muzzle at Joe, who had just broken leather with his pistol.

Joe's thumb fidgeted at the hammer, cocked it, but before he could squeeze the shot off, Owen fanned the hammer back once. Like Earl, the bullet struck Joe in the chest and exited his back near his spine.

Joe looked down at the hole in his chest and started to cough up blood. The pressure he'd been applying to the trigger was enough for it to fire.

Owen jerked in his saddle as the round grazed his side. "Argh!" he screamed. "You son of a bitch!" He fired his pistol again at Joe, knocking him from the saddle.

Earl was still on his horse, but dead, slumped over against the neck of the horse.

Owen touched his side and brought his hand forward to see it was covered in blood. "Damn it," he cursed.

Knowing he'd have to cut his day short to clean his wound, he headed directly for the Hartford's house.

HARTFORD RANCH, NOBLE COUNTY, OKLAHOMA TERRITORY

Owen rode up to find Allister chopping wood near the barn. He dismounted and immediately went to a trough of water to wash the blood from his hands and face.

Allister stopped what he was doing and stared, curious as to how the day had gone.

Clean, Owen walked his horse into the barn without

muttering a word or giving Allister even a glance.

Seeing Owen from the house, Franklin ran down and followed him into the barn. "Where did you go? What happened?"

"Two of the four bounty hunters you had coming won't be making it," Owen said, removing the saddle from his horse.

"Why?" Franklin asked.

"On account they're dead," Owen said, tossing the saddle on a railing. He tied a feed bag around his horse's head, flinching from the pain as he did it.

"You killed them?" Franklin asked.

"Yep, left them where they fell," Owen replied.

"Why in hell would you kill them?" Allister asked, entering the barn, his tone signaling he was irritated with the news.

"On account they were going to kill me. The second they heard who I was, they decided then and there they were going to collect the bounty that's on me!" Owen roared.

"Wait, you have a bounty on your head?" Franklin asked, shocked but also not too surprised by the announcement.

"When you're known as the Butcher of Bloody Creek, you tend to piss a few people off," Owen said.

Devious thoughts began to run through Allister's mind.

"So who were they, the bounty hunters you killed?" Franklin asked.

"I don't know, said their names were Earl and Joe,"

Owen said as he lifted up his shirt to reveal to them that he'd been shot.

"You're bleeding," Franklin gasped.

"Aren't you the smart one? A round grazed my side. I'll be fine; just need to clean it up and put a wrap on it."

"So now we're down to three men to do the job of five," Allister grunted.

"I can do this myself. Just trust me. I need to ride out later, finish getting the lay of the land. Once I do that, I'll be able to figure out how to get rid of your problem."

"It's not just our problem, it's yours; only difference is you're getting paid to do it," Allister snarked.

"Don't you worry, I'm heading back out later to scout. I needed to come back and get my side cleaned up," Owen replied, brushing past Franklin on his way to the house.

"Let me help you," Franklin said, jogging up next to him.

"Once you get cleaned up, get your ass back out there. I want them dead by the time the sun sets tomorrow," Allister crowed.

Owen stopped and turned back to face Allister. "It won't happen tomorrow. The earliest will be the day after that."

"But they're going to come looking for Terry," Allister snapped in anger.

"Good, better they come here, makes it easier for me," Owen said. He turned and headed back towards the house.

"And if they do, you'll still have to get the others, the

children too!" Allister hollered.

"Don't you worry your pretty little head. By the time the sun sets the day after tomorrow, they will all be dead," Owen replied.

MILKE HOMESTEAD, NOBLE COUNTY, OKLAHOMA TERRITORY

Oscar's son met the trio as they arrived at the homestead. He took Oscar's horse from him and asked, "Pa, who are they?"

"People who need our care," Oscar said.

Agatha exited the house and rushed to Oscar's side. "Who are these people?"

Whispering, Oscar replied, "Like I told Thomas, these people need our help. The woman is sick; I'm going to set them up in our shed."

"Is it the pox? Please tell me you didn't bring the pox here," Agatha said, placing her hand over her mouth in shock at the thought.

"She doesn't have the pox, but she's ill. Run inside and get blankets and a pillow. Thomas, go fetch a large bowl of water and some hand towels."

Oscar's other children, William and Elizabeth, emerged from the house and stared, excited to see strangers at the property.

Hurrying by them, Agatha chastised them. "No gawking, that's impolite."

"Who are they, Ma?" Elizabeth, the youngest, asked.

"Someone who needs our help, and what does the

good book say about helping those in need?" Agatha asked as she opened a steamer trunk and removed a thick wool blanket.

Both kids debated the biblical verse, both claiming they knew the correct response.

"Now stop the bickering," Agatha said.

"But, Ma…" William moaned. He was the middle child but relished being older than Elizabeth by almost two years.

"Never mind. Go get a basket and fill it with some of the bread I made yesterday," Agatha ordered.

The children did as they were asked and brought it to her.

"Thank you. Now go back to your studies. I expect that chalkboard to be full of answers to the equations I gave you," Agatha said.

The children groaned and walked away.

Agatha hurried to the shed to find Grady laying Abigail down on the dirt floor. "Oh, heavens no, let me lay this down. I have more blankets."

Grady lifted her back up and waited for Agatha, who promptly placed the thick blankets down.

With a softer and cleaner spot, he gently lowered Abigail to the ground.

Agatha stuffed a down pillow underneath her head. That was when she felt the heat radiating from Abigail. "Oh my, she's burning up."

"I know," Grady said.

"Thomas, hurry with that bowl of water!" Agatha hollered. Turning her attention back to Abigail, she asked

Grady, "What's her name?"

"Abigail, her name is Abigail," Grady replied.

Oscar showed as if on cue with a lantern; he hung it on a nail in the corner. The warm light from it cast over all in the small space. "How's she doing?"

Agatha felt cramped and could only imagine Abigail wouldn't like people hovering over her. "Can you all give her some space?"

Grady and Oscar nodded and exited without saying a word.

Abigail stirred and began to mumble. She opened her eyes and stared blankly at Agatha.

Agatha knelt next to Abigail and took her hand. "My dear, don't you fret. We're gonna get you better, you hear me?"

"Madeleine," Abigail muttered.

"Who's that? Is that your daughter?" Agatha asked.

"I promise," Abigail said, her head tossing back and forth.

A shadow cast over Agatha. She looked back and saw Thomas standing with his arms cradled around a large bowl of water. "Is she going to die?"

"Never mind that. Give me the bowl and those towels," she said, taking the bowl while nodding at the towels draped over his arm.

"Can I help with anything else?" Thomas asked.

"Make sure your siblings bring the bread," Agatha said, dipping a hand towel in the water. She wrung it out, folded it, and laid it tenderly on Abigail's forehead. Taking another, she did the same thing but instead used it to wipe off the hot sweat that covered Abigail's upper body and arms.

Thomas appeared again. "I got the bread."

"Just leave it," Agatha said.

Thomas did as she requested, but stood staring at Abigail's exposed torso.

Catching him, Agatha barked, "Away with you. Show this woman some respect."

Embarrassed, Thomas ran off.

"Sorry about my son. He's just curious," Agatha whispered.

"Madeleine," Abigail said again.

"We're going to get you better, okay; then you can go see this Madeleine you're talking about," Agatha said sweetly.

***

Agatha entered the house to find her children and Oscar sitting at the table, pensively waiting for news about Abigail. She looked around but didn't see Grady. "Where's the gentleman?"

"He went to Perry, had business there," Oscar replied.

Agatha filled a bowl with fresh water and washed her arms and hands. "Tell me how you came upon them?"

"I was returning from town after seeing if anyone had come across Terry, and saw their horses. I thought maybe the horses were—"

"Just get to the part where you invited these

gunfighters to our house," Agatha blurted out.

All eyes turned to Agatha.

"Gunfighters?" Oscar asked.

"That woman's body is covered in scars from cuts, gunshots, you name it. She was wearing a gun belt. I can't count how many knives, and that man, he isn't a businessman," Agatha said.

"I can only go off what the man told me," Oscar said, defending himself.

"You didn't think twice to look at how they were dressed? What did he say was his business?" Agatha asked.

"Prospector," Oscar replied.

"Prospecting what?" Agatha laughed.

"Iron ore, that's what he said, and you can't say you know if they do that here or not," Oscar said.

"I have never heard of mining for iron ore. I think he's lying to you," Agatha said, drying her hands.

"Then what should we do with them, with her?" Oscar asked.

"We're going to get her healthy; then they need to move on, but next time, please be more aware of who you're inviting onto our land," Agatha said, her nose scrunched.

"Would you have me let her die out there? You saw her condition," Oscar asked.

"Husband, I understand why you didn't. I'm just asking you think about who they might be first," Agatha said. "And children, stay clear of them both, you hear?"

In unison, all three children said, "Yes, Ma."

"Now I need you all to go run outside. I know you have some chores to complete," Agatha said to the children.

The children got up and exited the house, all complaining as they went.

When the door closed, Agatha asked, "What about Terry?"

"I need to go back out," he said, sitting at the table, his hands folded.

"I don't want you to go, with our guests here, but you have to go; we promised Pamela," Agatha said.

Oscar stood. He walked over to Agatha and took her in his arms. "I apologize for bringing these strangers here. At the time it felt like the right thing to do."

"It's fine, Oscar; you have a good heart and mean well," she replied.

He leaned in and kissed her lips. "Have Thomas keep an eye out, and you know where the shotgun is," he said.

"I'll be fine, now go; you're running out of daylight."

HARTFORD RANCH, NOBLE COUNTY, OKLAHOMA TERRITORY

Owen looked at the five playing cards in his hand then stared at the pile of coins in the center of the table. Having a pair of kings in his hand made him feel confident enough to call Allister's raise of ten dollars and up it by another ten.

"You must have a hell of a hand, or you're bluffing,"

Franklin said, tossing his cards in the middle. "All I know is I'm out."

"What about you?" Owen asked, looking at Allister.

Allister stared at his cards.

"Well, what are you going to do?" Owen pressed.

"I'll see that other ten," Allister replied, sliding a small stack of dollar coins into the heap of coins. "What do you have?"

Owen smiled and laid down his five cards. "Pair of kings."

Allister didn't budge. He sat emotionless and silent.

After waiting for a response, Owen leaned in to grab his winnings but stopped when Allister cried out, "Hold up."

Owen looked up and said, "Put them down if you got something."

"I believe a pair of aces beats a pair of kings," Allister said, laying his cards down, two aces at the top.

Frustrated that he'd lost, Owen slouched in his seat and said, "That's the third time tonight."

Sliding his winnings towards his side, Allister replied, "It appears I'm the lucky one here."

"Your brother doesn't cheat, does he?" Owen asked Franklin.

"Let's not start disparaging people just because you're getting beat," Allister said, a devilish grin stretched on his face. He delighted in the fact he was decisively beating Owen and relished seeing his stacks growing as Owen's were diminishing.

"Another hand?" Owen asked.

"Sure, I do believe it's Frank's turn to deal," Allister said.

"I'll deal, but I'm not playing. I've had enough losing for one night," Franklin said, scooping the cards up. He cradled them in his hand and began to shuffle.

"What's that noise?" Owen asked, quickly drawing his pistol from its holster.

"Noise, what noise?" Franklin asked. He stopped shuffling and listened.

Allister hadn't heard it either. He slowly turned around, only to be startled when someone began to bang on the door.

Owen cocked his pistol and placed it on the table, his hand still firmly on the grip.

Franklin and Allister exchanged a quick glance.

"Who's there?"

"My name is Grady. I'm looking for a Mr. Hartford. I was told I could find him here."

Whispering, Allister asked Franklin, "Who's Grady?"

"He must be another hired gun. I told you I had two more coming," Franklin replied. He jumped to his feet and went to the door. Opening it, he found Grady standing with his hands planted firmly on his hips. "Evening."

"Are you Hartford?" Grady asked. He peeked over Franklin's shoulder and took note there were two others in the room.

"I'm Franklin Hartford. Are you responding to the query about some hired guns?"

"I am," Grady answered.

"Come on in," Franklin said, swinging the door open fully. "Anyone else with you?"

"I have a partner," Grady replied.

"Where is he?" Franklin asked, looking around outside.

"Not here on account of feeling under the weather," Grady said, stepping inside the house. He nodded to Allister then to Owen. When he got a good look at Owen, he asked, "You look familiar. Do I know you?"

"I don't know, do I?" Owen replied.

Grady caught sight of Owen holding the pistol and said, "There's no need for that. I'm here to inquire about the job and get what information I can on it."

Owen decocked the pistol and holstered it.

"Take a seat," Franklin said, motioning to a chair opposite Owen.

Grady sat and asked, "You all playing cards? Deal me in."

"Where do you come from?" Allister asked.

"Texas," Grady answered.

Franklin sat back down and said, "I suppose you'd like to know about the job."

"Yeah, I would," Grady said. "We rode all the way from Paris, so I pray the job is still available."

"Oh, it is. We need some extra bodies to get it done," Allister snarked, hoping to get under Owen's skin a bit.

"All I know is we need to run off some squatters. Doesn't sound too hard," Grady said.

Allister burst out into laughter. "Run off?"

Grady furrowed his brow and asked, "Is something funny?"

"Want me to tell or you?" Allister asked Franklin.

"You go ahead," Franklin replied.

"Son, you're here to get rid of squatters for us, that's correct, but we need them killed."

"Killed? Hmm, I didn't read that about the job," Grady said, confused.

"Are you a greenhorn or something?" Owen snapped at Grady.

Grady whipped his head around to look at Owen and answered, "I swear I know you. Who are you?" He faced Franklin and continued, "Who is he? 'Cause he looks very familiar."

Owen placed his elbows on the table and said, "I'm Owen Blake, but you probably know me as the Butcher of Bloody Creek."

Leaning in as well, Grady stared intently at Owen and said, "Nope, never heard of you." Of course he was lying, but he knew his response would irritate Owen, who was prideful of his notorious reputation.

"You've never heard of Owen Blake, the Butcher of Bloody Creek?" Franklin asked, shocked.

"No, sir, never heard of him. Where is Bloody Creek? Is that a town or an actual creek somewhere?" Grady asked, hoping to taunt Owen more.

"I killed dozens of Indian savages back in—"

"Wait, hold on, I think…ah, nope, never heard of it. Anyway, you're Franklin Hartford, and you're…?" Grady asked Allister.

"I'm his brother, Allister."

"Nice to meet you, so let's get back to the job. You need these squatters killed?"

"Yes," Allister answered.

"How many are we talking about?" Grady asked, undeterred about the job so far only because he considered squatters lowlifes.

"Thirteen," Franklin replied.

"Most of them women and children," Allister added.

Grady raised his brow, shocked by the admission. "You want me to kill women and children?"

"They're squatters all the same. They're here on my land and I want them off," Allister replied.

Knowing he couldn't refuse the job then and there for fear he could put himself in an awkward position, he decided to play along and, when the timing was right, leave and not come back.

"Do you have the stomach for such a thing?" Allister asked.

"Sure do. Killing squatters is no different than squashing cockroaches, if you ask me," Grady said.

"Good, you'll be working alongside Owen—" Allister said but was interrupted.

"I work alone," Owen barked.

Ignoring Owen, Grady asked, "Give me the details of who needs killin' and where I can find them. I'll start first thing in the morning."

"You just stay out of my way," Owen snarled.

"Mr. Blake, there's more than enough for both of us to take care of. How about we come to some sort of arrangement?"

"That's a good idea," Allister said.

"I don't work with anyone, period," Owen growled, his temper flaring.

"How about we go outside and talk?" Franklin proposed to Grady.

With a wicked grin gracing his face, Grady got to his feet and said, "Good idea. No need to deal me in."

Franklin led him outside. The sun was nearing the horizon and soon darkness would come.

Grady wondered how Abigail was doing. He'd often thought about her since leaving her with Oscar and his family.

Escorting him away from the house for more privacy, Franklin jumped right into the heart of the matter. "Are you sure you're fine with what we're needing done?"

"You must mean the killing of women and children part?" Grady joked.

"Yes."

"I can say that I'm not one who enjoys such things, but please let me know the specifics of the job," Grady said.

"There are three families who have squatted on our land. We've tried many times to negotiate with them, but they won't leave. They're declaring they have a superior claim to ours, and no one at the land office will listen," Franklin said. He took a deep breath and exhaled. "My brother and I have plans for this land, but we can't see it through until they're gone."

"Why not just get a bigger force and run them off? Killing is kind of harsh, specifically the women and children part," Grady opened up.

"My brother insists on it," Franklin confessed.

"So your brother is the one calling the shots?" Grady asked.

Franklin cringed; he hated when he heard how his brother was the boss of him. "This is the job. Do you want it or not?"

"Let me talk to my partner. I'll get back to you first thing in the morning," Grady said. "I do apologize, as I usually don't reconsider jobs. It's just that you were vague in the description of what needed to be done."

"And for that I'm the one who needs to be sorry. It didn't feel right sending a telegram saying we were contracting killers," Franklin said.

Grady looked up at the sun as it disappeared and knew he had a good forty-minute ride ahead of him. He tipped his hat and said, "Have a good evening. I'll talk to you tomorrow."

"Good night, Mr.?"

"Just call me Grady."

"Then good night, Grady," Franklin said.

Grady jumped on his horse and rode away. He had no plans of coming back to see Franklin or the other men. He was less concerned about the jobs he took, but knew Abigail was more discerning; there was no way she'd ever accept a job where the job description was killing women and children. What bothered him most was how she'd look at him. He'd convinced her to ride for three days only to find out the job was unacceptable. Had he just blown his chance with her?

Franklin watched Grady ride off. He wasn't sure what to make of him, but something told him he wasn't coming back.

Allister emerged from the house and walked up alongside Franklin. As he packed his pipe with fresh tobacco, he asked, "That fella isn't coming back, is he?"

"I don't think so," Franklin confessed, his thinning hair blowing in the cool breeze.

"No need to worry. I'll have this all handled by myself very soon," Owen said, leaning up against the doorjamb.

Allister turned around and said, "You keep saying that. You seem like a man who likes to talk."

"You can take my word to the bank," Owen said.

"We shall see," Allister said. "Now, how about we go back inside? I'm itching to beat you at poker again."

JONES HOMESTEAD, NOBLE COUNTY, OKLAHOMA TERRITORY

Oscar sat in the saddle of his horse just down the trail that led to Terry's house. He could see Pamela through a window, no doubt making supper for the children and most certainly worrying about her husband.

He'd met with Robert, but the second after he'd divulged his fears about Terrence, all he got back from Robert was dismay. Robert's response disheartened Oscar and left him despondent. What was he going to say to

Pamela? Agatha was insistent that he tell her what he knew, but he knew that would lead him to a confrontation with the Hartford brothers, something he wasn't longing to have happen in light of losing his base of support.

What would he tell Agatha if he returned without talking to Pamela? How could he stand tall like the man of the house knowing he'd lied to her? This was something he couldn't run from. He needed to tell Pamela his credible suspicions and follow through, knowing he'd now have to do it alone.

Filled with mixed feelings and emotions running high, he nudged his horse forward and towards Terry's house.

Pamela spotted Oscar riding up and ran out of the house to confront him. "I've been worried sick all day. Have you heard anything?"

Oscar dismounted. He took her by the arm and said, "Let's go talk inside the house."

Her body grew rigid from fear. "What's happened to my Terrence?"

"Please, let's go talk inside," he urged.

Her children stepped outside and looked at them both.

Catching the children's curious gazes, Oscar knew the house was not the correct venue. "Children, best you go inside. I need to discuss something with your mother."

Pamela's legs felt weak. "Is he dead?"

The children didn't budge.

Raising his voice, Oscar barked, "Inside the house."

Obedient, the children disappeared into the house and closed the door behind them.

"Let's go sit down on that log," Oscar said, taking her by the arm.

She sat down and nervously smoothed out her skirt. "Don't you beat around the bush, Oscar Milke, just tell me straight. What's befallen my Terrence?"

Taking a seat next to her, Oscar told her about the conversation he'd had with Terry in town, then described his suspicions to her.

"I knew he was hardheaded, I knew it. He went to confront those brothers and got himself killed, didn't he?"

"I don't know for sure. I've gone and met the others and I've been to town. No one has seen Terry. I can only assume he went to visit them and something awful happened."

She sprang to her feet. "I'll just ride over there myself and find out."

Taking her hand, he pulled her back down and said, "You won't do that. I won't allow it."

"You're not the boss of me, Oscar. My husband is missing, and what you're telling me is he's been killed by those Hartford brothers."

"It's only a hunch," Oscar said.

"A credible one and one I mean to find out if it's true," she snapped.

"If Terry was killed, then the last thing your children need is their mother ending up with the same fate," Oscar said.

"Someone needs to confront them," she barked.

"I will; I'll ride over," Oscar said.

"And what will I say to Agatha if you get killed?" Pamela asked.

"Then what are you proposing?"

"It's my cross to bear, Oscar. I appreciate what you're offering to do, but it's my fight," Pamela said, her temperament shifting as determination grounded her footing.

"No, I'll go; I'll leave now," Oscar said.

Taking his arm, she squeezed it and said, "No, I won't allow it. What I do need from you, though, is to take my children home with you."

"You're going right this minute? Why not wait until morning? What if I accompanied you?" Oscar asked.

Pamela paused as she thought.

"What do you say?" he asked.

"What did Robert say?" Pamela asked.

"He's taken a step back from our agreement. He's scared," Oscar replied.

"Rightfully so," Pamela said, showing she wasn't angry with Robert for shifting his position.

"The thing is, Pamela, we don't know if Terry went over there. Like I said, it's just a hunch," Oscar said.

She touched his face and said, "You and I both know he went over there. I've known Terry for many years, and in those years he often allowed his temper to get the better of him."

Oscar stood and said, "I'll come back in the morning."

"Very well," Pamela said, though she really wasn't committed to doing what he wanted.

Oscar bid her farewell and left. As he rode away, he prayed she wasn't lying and that she'd stay put until tomorrow.

MILKE HOMESTEAD, NOBLE COUNTY, OKLAHOMA TERRITORY

Unable to curb his curiosity, Thomas snuck out of the house and went to check on Abigail. At first he tried to peek through gaps in the siding but couldn't really see, so he found the courage to open the door and poke his head in.

Abigail lay silently, her chest rising and lowering with each breath she took.

He was fascinated by her, especially after hearing his mother say that she and Grady were probably gunslingers. He'd read about the mysterious and dangerous gunslingers who inhabited the west, and now he was face-to-face with some.

He opened the door farther to get a look at her gun belt, which hung from a nail on the wall; however, he was unaware there was a pail just behind the door. When he pushed the door more, it knocked the pail over and made a loud crash.

Spooked, he tried to exit, but Abigail was now awake.

"Who is that?" Abigail asked.

Caught, Thomas decided to take the moment and

make it a positive. "I'm sorry. I came to check on you, to see if you needed anything. I accidentally knocked over…"

"That's okay," Abigail said.

"Um, how are you feeling?" Thomas asked.

Abigail fully rolled over and replied, "I feel a tad better for sure."

"That's good. I'll let my mother and father know," he said, smiling sheepishly.

"What's your name?" Abigail asked.

"Thomas."

"Hi, Thomas, my name is Abigail, in case you didn't know," she said.

Unable to control himself, he blurted out, "Are you gunslingers?"

Abigail chuckled. "No, we're not gunslingers per se."

Disappointed, he asked, "Then why carry a pistol like that?"

"Everyone should carry a weapon. You never know who or what you might come upon," she answered honestly.

"Ma doesn't like guns," he confessed.

"Well, I'm sure she has her reasons," Abigail said.

"Says they're evil," Thomas said.

"They can be in the wrong hands. I look at it this way, a gun is a tool; it's as good or bad as the person wielding it."

Thomas contemplated what she just said and asked, "Ma doesn't believe you're here prospecting. She thinks you and your friend are gunslingers."

"Prospectors?" Abigail said then realized this must be a cover story Grady had given the family. Wanting to change the topic, she asked, "When did you all get to Oklahoma?"

"Weeks ago, it was a tough trip, but Pa said there was opportunity out here. That it was a place a man could create his own way and be something. He was so happy until…"

Sensing something was wrong, she pressed, "Until what?"

"I shouldn't be talking to you," Thomas said, taking a step to exit the shed.

"Are you all in trouble or something?" she asked.

"It's those brothers, they're giving Pa a hard time. This is our land and, well…"

"Don't say any more," she said. "Best you get back inside before your ma misses you."

"Sorry I woke you," Thomas said.

"It's fine and, Thomas," she said.

He looked at her, anxious to hear what she was going to say.

"Thank you. Your family is generous and kind; it's something that one should appreciate when they come upon it."

"You're welcome, and good night," Thomas said, closing the door. As he walked the distance back to the house, he was startled by Grady riding in. "Evening."

Grady dismounted and asked, "Why are you out here in the dark?"

"I went to go check on Abigail. She's doing fine, by

the way. You know, at first I thought you were Pa," Thomas answered.

"Where's your Pa?" Grady asked.

"Oh, he—" Thomas said before being interrupted by his mother, who opened the door to the house and called out.

"Thomas, get inside here," Agatha snapped.

"Sorry, Ma, I went outside to—"

"Go fetch some water. Your brother and sister need it for their bath," Agatha said. Seeing Grady, she said to him, "Good evening, Mr. Grady."

Grady replied, "Your son said Abigail is feeling better."

Agatha glared at Thomas and barked, "Who said you could go visit her?"

Upset that he'd been outed, Thomas replied, "I didn't mean any harm."

"I can't thank you and your husband enough for taking us in," Grady said.

"Well, that's what good Christian people do," she said, giving him a wary glare.

Sensing she felt uneasy around him, he excused himself. "I'm going to go see to Abigail. Thank you again." He turned around and walked away.

"I imagine you're hungry," she called out.

Grady stopped and turned to face her. "I could use a bite for sure." He hoped that meant inviting him in for supper.

"I'll have Thomas bring a plate over to you in a bit," Agatha said.

Tipping his hat, Grady said, "Much obliged, ma'am."

Agatha went inside the house and closed the door, leaving Grady totally in the dark.

Grady went to the shed, tied up his horse, and took its saddle off. Inside, he found Abigail lying peacefully under the comforting glow of the lantern. He knelt next to her and checked her forehead with the back of his hand. "Your fever is down."

Abigail stirred.

He retracted his hand and sat back, leaning against the rough wood wall.

Opening her eyes, Abigail blinked repeatedly until she cleared her vision. "Grady, is that you?" she asked, her voice cracking.

Leaning in, he replied, "Yeah. I didn't mean to wake you."

"I was awake already. I'm just lying here," she said.

"How are you feeling?"

"Better," she answered.

"It feels like your fever is down," he said, his rigid expression melting away to expose a softer side.

Abigail's eyes looked around the small space. "Where are we?"

"Somewhere safe," he replied.

She lifted her head but stopped short of going further.

Seeing she was struggling, he said, "Ease up. You need to rest."

"I know we're at someone's home, but where are we?"

"Just outside Perry," he answered.

"And the job?" she asked.

"Don't worry about that," he said.

She sighed and said, "I don't know what happened. I'm sorry, but I do feel like I'm getting better."

"No, no, no, don't you dare feel sorry. Stuff happens. You got sick is all, and by the looks of it, you're already coming back."

The small door of the shed creaked open. Thomas stuck his head in and said, "I got supper."

Abigail gave him a sweet look and said, "Hello, Thomas."

Thomas stepped fully into the shed and said, "Oh, hello, Mr. Grady, here's your supper."

"Thank you," Grady said.

"Will you be needin' food too?" Thomas asked Abigail.

"Can you eat?" Grady asked her.

"I am hungry," Abigail replied.

Grady took the plate from Thomas. "Go get another plate for me."

Thomas nodded and rushed off.

Grady placed the plate on the floor and reached behind Abigail. "Can you sit up?"

"Yeah," Abigail said. While she slowly rose, he stuffed the pillow behind her to give her support.

"Good?" he asked.

"Yes, that's perfect," she said, giving him a slight grin.

Taking the spoon in his hand, Grady scooped up a

small spoonful of grits and said, "There's melted butter on this." He brought the spoon to her lips.

Before she opened her mouth, she said, "Smells so good."

"Eat up. Get your strength back," he said.

She opened her mouth and ate the spoonful without any problem.

He scooped up a more generous portion and fed her.

She ate that without problem.

"You're hungry." He laughed.

"I am," she said.

He fed her until the plate was empty.

Thomas arrived with another plate and handed it to him. "Will you be needing more?"

"If you have more, bring it," Grady said.

Like before, Thomas hurried away.

Grady mixed the butter thoroughly into the grits and filled the spoon. "Open up."

Abigail shook her head and said, "No, you eat."

"I'm fine. I need you to get back on your feet."

Giving in, she opened her mouth and took another spoonful. As she chewed, she smiled at him, her eyes sparkling.

Grady noticed her gaze and matched it with his.

"Thank you," Abigail said.

"For what?"

Lowering her head, she answered, "You made sure I was taken care of. And now you're feeding me like a child."

"We're partners." He smiled.

"I am sorry, I'm not being a partner to you; we have a job to do and I'm here, sick and unable to do anything," Abigail lamented.

"Abby, don't worry about it. It's not like there's a job to do anyway," he said, letting slip a clue to the job.

"What does that mean?" she asked.

He sat upright and answered, "I spoke to the gentleman who put the call out for the job." He sighed and continued, "We can't take it."

Sitting up higher, she asked, "Why not?"

"On account they don't want muscle to move squatters, they want hired guns to kill…kill women and children."

Her eyes widened at the revelation.

"What are you saying?" she asked.

"They want us to kill these squatters, all of them, including the women and the children," he answered.

"What did you tell them?" she asked.

Grady paused and thought before answering. Regret filled his heart. "I'm the one who's sorry. I brought you all the way up here for nothing. I won't do what they're asking, and I know you won't either."

Hearing his response gave her ease. She relaxed and said, "It's fine. We'll find another job."

A smile creased his face. "You're not mad?"

"Why would I be mad? You made the right call," she said.

He exhaled heavily and said, "I was so worried you'd be mad at me for dragging you all the way up here for nothing."

"I'd be mad at you if you tried to convince me to take the job," she said.

Both grew silent when the sound of a galloping horse hit their ears.

Grady put the plate down and said, "Must be Oscar."

Abigail smiled, took the plate, and said, "Go ahead."

Grady exited the shed to find Oscar dismounting. "Hey there."

Oscar looked but couldn't see Grady through the black of night. "Grady?"

"It's me," Grady answered, walking towards him.

"Now I see you," Oscar said when Grady appeared from the shadows. "Walk with me to the barn."

The two men walked together, both exchanging small talk.

Inside the barn, Oscar lit a lantern. The orange flame illuminated the space.

"Where did you go?" Grady asked.

As Oscar unbuckled the horse's saddle, he said, "Just dealing with some business." Switching topics, he continued, "I let you onto my land. My family is inside that house, vulnerable to some extent. So tell me, truthfully, what are you doing here? Because I know it's not prospecting for iron ore."

Stunned by the question, Grady again tried to lie. "It's true, me and my partner are here to—"

Tossing the saddle over a beam, Oscar turned and snapped, "Cut the bull. My wife saw through you the second she laid eyes on you and your female friend. You're not prospectors at all; you're gunfighters, maybe even bounty hunters or, worse, hired guns."

Grady chuckled.

"You find that funny?" Oscar asked, squaring up to Grady.

"Your wife, she's got a good eye," Grady said.

"So she's correct, you're gunfighters? Tell me, what are gunfighters doing in Perry?" Oscar asked.

"We were hired to run off some squatters," Grady confessed.

When the word *squatter* hit Oscar's ears, he stepped back, fearing that he could be standing face-to-face with a man hired to kill him.

Noticing his reaction, Grady said, "I didn't take the job after I heard the specifics."

"And those were?" Oscar asked.

"I don't want to get graphic, but the job wasn't what I expected it to be, and my partner, Abby, she'd never have done it."

"Care to tell me who hired you?" Oscar asked.

"A man by the name of Franklin Hartford. He sent—"

Interrupting him, Oscar gasped. "Franklin hired you to kill us."

"I never said anything about killing."

"You didn't have to say it. This is Franklin and Allister we're talking about; I know those men," Oscar blared, taking a few steps away from Grady. He placed his right hand on his pistol and said, "You get out of here, go."

Grady raised his hands high and said, "Easy now. I

told you the truth and I don't have any intention of helping them. Abby and I didn't travel all this way to murder people, specifically women and children."

"He wants to kill my wife and children?" Oscar asked, shocked by the revelation.

"Yes, sir, and that's why we're not taking the job. Now you need to understand that there's another man they have employed, and he's a mean and ruthless son of a bitch. I met him tonight, and I expect him to come for you soon, maybe as early as the morning."

"Someone is coming to kill my family in the morning?" Oscar asked.

"I don't know for sure when, but you should expect it; heck, he might show tonight," Grady said.

Wide eyed and filled with fear to the point of trembling, Oscar pushed past Grady and ran out of the barn.

Grady followed him out but instead went to the shed. It was time to move on regardless of Abigail's condition. Reaching the shed, he found her lying where he'd left her before.

The second she saw the look on his face, she knew something was wrong. "What's happened?"

"The squatters we were hired to kill, Oscar and his family are them," Grady said.

"And Oscar knows…everything?" Abigail asked, sitting up further.

"Yeah."

"These are good people. They helped me when I needed it," Abigail said.

"I think we should leave," Grady said.

"We're not going to leave these people, we're going to help them," Abigail declared.

"But they're squatters. I don't think we should get involved," Grady said.

"They helped me," Abigail said.

Commotion outside tore Grady away from the conversation. He stuck his head out of the shed and could see the front door of the house was open.

"Agatha, I don't care. Just gather what you can!" Oscar hollered, running down to the barn.

Abigail struggled but eventually got to her feet. She hobbled over to Grady and braced her weight against him.

He turned and said, "They're heading out."

"Get out of my way," Abigail said, pushing Grady out of the way and exiting the shed. "Agatha!" Abigail cried out.

Hearing her name being called, Agatha looked and saw Abigail slowly coming towards her. "You stay away from me and my family, you hear me."

"I'm not here to harm you or your family. I just need to talk," Abigail said.

"You stay where you are!" Agatha barked.

"I can help, both me and Grady can help; I just need to know what's going on," Abigail said. She had listened to Agatha and hadn't approached closer.

"You're with those evil men, aren't you?" Agatha blared.

"No, we're not; we came because we heard about a

job, but we didn't take it. I just need to know what the truth is," Abigail said.

Grady came up behind Abigail and asked, "What are you doing, Abby? These people are squatters."

"No, they're not. Look at them. They're just a family who probably came from far away to start a new life, and now someone is aiming to take what's theirs."

"You don't know that," Grady said.

Cutting him a harsh look, Abigail snapped, "Any man who would call for the killing of innocents, of children, is not someone who can be trusted. That's a man trying to steal and cover his tracks completely."

Grady hadn't thought of it that way before.

Putting her attention back on Agatha, who still remained in the doorway, Abigail asked, "It's that Hartford man, he's the squatter, isn't he?"

From the darkness came the answer. "He is," Oscar said, emerging from the shadows and into the light of the open doorway.

"I figured as much. Let me see if I can summarize. You claimed this land fair and square while Mr. Hartford didn't; he just came and set up without any legal authority."

"You're doing a lot of guessing," Grady said.

"It's called intuition," Abigail replied to Grady.

"That's all correct what you're saying about Franklin Hartford and his brother, Allister," Oscar said.

"We need to help these people," Abigail said to Grady.

Taking her by the arm, he leaned in. "You're still not

well; in fact, I'm beginning to think you're delirious."

She shrugged him off and said, "You can leave anytime you want."

Overhearing Abigail and Grady bicker, Oscar approached cautiously. "How can you help us?"

Abigail took a few steps closer to Oscar and said, "I'm pretty damn good behind a gun."

"You're willing to fight for us?" Oscar asked.

"Not fight for you as some sort of proxy, but fight alongside you—there's a difference," Abigail said.

"You're willing to do that?" Oscar asked, showing how confused he was in the creases of his face.

"Yes, sir," Abigail said, determined and standing tall though she was feeling a surge of weakness begin to rise in her.

"Why?" Oscar asked.

"On account I can tell you're good people. You took me in when I was sick—"

"You're still sick," Grady blared, interrupting her.

Ignoring Grady, she continued, "On account you took me in. You didn't ask, you just opened your house, fed me, cared for me. Your wife even gave me a cold-water bath. You came out here to begin something new and have come face-to-face with the sort of people I've been fighting for years."

"What do you need from us?" Oscar asked.

"Do you want to keep your land?" Abigail asked.

"I do…we do," Oscar answered.

"Then fight for it. If you do that, I'll stand side by side with you," Abigail said, putting her hand out.

Oscar gave Agatha a wary look.

Agatha still stood in the doorway, her hand over her heart, shocked by the exchange.

Putting his attention back on Abigail, Oscar said, "I'll stand and fight for my land."

"Then you have a partner," Abigail said.

Oscar took her hand and shook. "Thank you."

Grady growled his disappointment under his breath.

"And your partner?" Oscar asked.

Abigail turned around and said, "Grady, I understand that this isn't your fight, but you know me. This is the purpose God gave me long ago."

"You're allowing what happened to that family days ago to cloud your judgment," Grady challenged.

"No, I'm doing exactly what I did that day; I'm standing up for good people. What you're doing, though, is the same; you're hesitant, you're only thinking of yourself."

"I'm not. I just don't know the truth here. How do we know he's not lyin'?" Grady asked.

"I'm not lying," Oscar said staunchly.

"A man that takes me in isn't a thief; a woman who tenderly cares for me doesn't steal so arrogantly; however, a man who would have children killed is a man who would steal from the Pope himself."

Grady thought about what she said before walking up alongside her. "It's only because I trust your intuition that I say yes."

"Are you sure?" Abigail asked.

"I go where you go," Grady said.

Abigail faced Oscar and said, "You'll have our guns to back you up when need be."

"Thank you," Oscar said. He turned to Agatha. "We're not leaving; we're here to stay."

"I'll go tell the children," Agatha said, disappearing into the house.

"There's a couple of other families that I've agreed to stand up for. I'll ride over to them in the morning and let them know we have an ally."

"Good, now if you'll excuse me, I need to go lie down," Abigail said. She nodded and slowly walked back towards the shed.

Grady caught up to her and said, "I've never met anyone like you in my life."

"Is that a compliment?" she asked.

"It is," he said.

She clutched his forearm and sighed.

"Are you okay?" he asked.

"I need to go lie down. That took the wind out of my sails," she replied.

"Come, let me help you back," he said, putting his arm around her. With his help, she walked back to the shed.

Lying down again, she exhaled heavily and said, "I need to rest."

"You do that," he said, getting to his feet.

"Where are you going?" she asked.

"To find a place to sleep," he replied.

"There's room enough in here," she said.

"You need rest, and my snoring might keep you up.

Good night, Abigail," he said, tipping his hat.

"Good night, Grady," she said then closed her eyes.

Outside, Grady looked up at the starlit sky and pondered what he'd just gotten himself involved in. Fighting was not something he shied away from, but going up against a man like Owen Blake was definitely something that gave him pause.

CHAPTER FIVE

HARTFORD RANCH, NOBLE COUNTY, OKLAHOMA TERRITORY

OCTOBER 11, 1893

Pamela had given her children specific instructions to only ride to the Milke homestead if she hadn't returned by noon. She didn't know what would happen, but after sleeping on it, she couldn't have Oscar also risking his life. If Terrence had gone to see the Hartford brothers, then it was her business to verify.

Her hands gripped the reins tightly as she rode up to the front of the house.

The sun hadn't risen yet, but the light of the new day coming gave her enough to see.

The front door opened and out stepped Franklin. "Is that you, Mrs. Jones?"

Pamela pulled back on the reins and stopped her horse from advancing. "Franklin, good morning."

Hearing the conversation, Allister exited the house. He walked past Franklin, cocked his head and asked, "What can we do for ya, Mrs. Jones?"

"I'd like to talk to you...both," she replied. "But first, can you put on something more appropriate?" she said, referring to Allister's attire being simply long underwear.

"Of course. May we offer you coffee with chicory?"

Allister asked.

"That sounds fine," Pamela said, dismounting the horse.

"Care to come inside?" Franklin asked.

Goose bumps covered her skin, and the hair on the back of her neck was raised. She looked around the front and said, "You know, it's such a wonderful morning, I think I'll just sit over there near that lovely tree."

"Sure thing," Franklin said.

The two met at the tree. Next to the trunk sat a single chair. It was where Allister would come and sit in the evenings sometimes and smoke his pipe.

"It's a nice view, isn't it?" Franklin asked.

"It is," she said, trying to make sure her voice didn't crack from the fear.

"Please take a seat," Franklin offered. He had no doubt she was there to see about her husband. Just how he or Allister would handle that pending question was what lingered doubtfully with him.

Allister emerged from the house, dressed and carrying two cups of steaming coffee. He walked up and said, "Here you go."

Pamela reached for it with her trembling hands.

Seeing her hands, Allister knew he had the upper hand. "I have to say, Mrs. Jones, you being here without your husband is quite peculiar."

"I've come to negotiate," she said.

"Negotiate?" Allister asked.

"Yes. You offered my husband something for our land a few weeks back. I'd like to see if that offer is still available."

Franklin and Allister both raised their brows.

"Is it?" she asked, taking a small sip of the coffee.

"Depends," Allister replied.

"On what?" she asked.

"The terms have changed. I offered to buy the land for a fair price, but your husband would have to work it for me in exchange for living there."

"How have the terms changed?" she asked.

Allister gave her an odd look and asked, "Why are you really here?"

"I'm here to negotiate you buying our land," she said.

"Why isn't Terry here?" Allister asked, clearly knowing the answer but curious about how she'd respond.

"I'm afraid that Terry is gone. He left us; abandoned would be the better way to say it," she said.

"Oh, he did? I'm so sorry to hear that." Allister snickered.

"Mr. Hartford, are you interested in my land or not?" she asked.

Exiting the house, Owen glanced over and sneered at the three. He couldn't hear what they were saying, but all he could see was money going away.

Catching a glimpse of Owen, Pamela choked a bit on a sip of coffee and began to cough.

"Are you okay?" Franklin asked.

"Who is that man?" she replied.

Looking back, Franklin answered, "That's—"

"Don't pay no mind to him, ma'am. Now I see it this way; you want to make the same deal as I offered to your husband weeks ago, but it appears we can't on account that he's done up and left you and your kids."

"Don't you dare say one bad word about my Terry," she spat.

"Now, Mrs. Jones, how come you're here defending your lowlife husband, who up and abandoned you?" Allister continued. He was enjoying watching her squirm.

She shot up and handed the cup to Franklin. "I won't sit here and be subject to insults targeted at my husband."

"Hold on, just wait. How much are you willing to take for your land?" Allister asked. He would pay it if the amount was less than what he had to pay to Owen.

"What was the offer to Terrence?" she asked.

"Two hundred plus he would stay on and work the land," Allister answered as he picked his teeth with the tip of his knife.

Repulsed by Allister, she countered, "Three hundred and no questions asked and no questions ever answered. I'll pack up my children and head back to Ohio, never to speak of this place ever again."

"Hmm, how about two hundred and fifty?" Allister asked.

"Mr. Hartford, you're getting more than just the land, you're also getting the house and the outbuildings."

"Two seventy-five, then," he fired back.

"Three fifteen and you can keep all the livestock and equipment. It's a turnkey operation for you."

Allister smiled and shot Franklin a look. "What do you think, little brother?"

"Sounds like a fair deal," Franklin answered.

"Three fifteen it is," Allister said, holding his hand out to her.

"I don't need to shake your hand. Just write it up, and have the money ready. After that, we'll be on our way," she said.

"You heard her, little brother. Go draft a contract and get the money," Allister ordered.

Franklin rushed off.

"Can I offer you a bite to eat while you wait?" Allister asked.

"No, I'm not staying."

Confused, Allister asked, "Where are you going? I thought we were going to complete this transaction?"

"Listen here, Mr. Hartford, I don't trust you, not one bit. I won't be signing a damn thing here while I'm vulnerable to your actions. You're to deliver that to the land office today with the money. There I'll sign it and take my money."

Allister grinned and said, "You're a smart woman, you know that, Mrs. Jones. I can see what Terry saw in you."

Not wanting to even address his latest comment, she scowled and said, "Good day, Mr. Hartford, and may you rot in hell."

Laughing heartedly, he replied, "Good day to you too."

Pamela hurried back to her horse, passing Owen on

the way, and mounted it.

Owen cast a sinister look her way before turning to Allister. "We need to talk."

Needing to go before she vomited, Pamela turned the horse around and galloped off.

"What am I doing here?" Owen asked.

"Getting rid of the squatters who don't want to make deals like this smart woman here," Allister said.

"Then why didn't you make deals with them before hiring me?" Owen asked.

"I tried to; they didn't take them," Allister answered.

"That looked quite easy," Owen said.

"On account she knows I killed her husband, and she's doing what she feels is best for her family outside of getting killed. That woman there is not only brave but one of the savviest ladies I've ever met. She has more balls than most men, coming in here like she did. Very impressive woman," Allister said.

Franklin came out of the house and said, "Contract is drafted. Where's Mrs. Jones?"

"She left. Take that to town; drop it off at the land office along with the money. Make sure you get our deed for that land," Allister ordered.

Surprised by the sudden turn of events, Franklin nodded and said, "Whatever you say, brother." He turned and went back inside the house.

"And, Owen, let's make one thing clear; you're not in charge here. If you want to up and leave, then go. I won't be threatened by the hired help."

Owen seethed.

"Now how about doing what I did hire you for and finish off those other two families," Allister said before disappearing into the house.

JONES HOMESTEAD, NOBLE COUNTY, OKLAHOMA TERRITORY

Oscar lay in bed all night thinking about the positive developments of having Abigail and Grady on their side. He couldn't wait to tell Pamela, so when he arrived at the Jones homestead to find Pamela packing a wagon, he was taken aback.

"Where are you going?" Oscar asked.

"We're leaving," she simply answered.

"Leaving, no, no, you can't," he said.

"I met with Allister Hartford this morning," she said.

"You did what? I told you to wait for me," he said.

Pamela stopped what she was doing and looked down at her dust-covered shoes. All around her was open land with tall grasses. She was in the middle of nowhere and now without a husband. The dreams of the family could not be the same without Terry around, and she knew justice was not going to happen. Distraught, she said, "I know he killed Terry, I know it; yet I can't prove it. How do I prove he killed my Terry, huh?" Tears began to well up. "Coming here was a dream Terry and I had together, but with him gone, how do I run a ranch? I don't know anything about it. How am I supposed to keep my children safe?"

Her words instantly made him think about Grady

and Abigail and how they'd been hired to kill everyone, including the children.

"The second I saw that man this morning, I knew, I just knew he'd killed Terry."

"How did you confront him about it?" he asked.

"I didn't. At first I thought about riding over there and shooting him; then I thought about the children and what you told me about leaving them without any parent. Even if I had killed Allister, I wouldn't have been able to kill the other two."

She was clearly referring to Franklin and the man Owen whom Grady had mentioned.

"I woke this morning more determined than ever to avenge Terry, but the closer I drew, the more I looked at this foreign land I'm living in. This isn't my home. I don't want my children to grow up here. We tried to make a go, but I can't risk their lives; and believe me when I say that Allister Hartford is a threat to be reckoned with. No, the second I saw him, I knew he'd killed Terry, and I also knew that I was going to sell him my land."

"Sell? No, Pamela, please tell me you didn't sell?" Oscar cried out. "I have a plan. We have others that will help us."

She took his hands and said, "I don't want to live here anymore. This clearly was more Terry's dream than mine. I don't want this, any of it."

"Then why didn't you sell to me?" Oscar asked.

"On account I got top dollar going to him. I did what was best for my family, and if that upsets you…let's just say I can't worry about such trivial things," she said.

"Oh, Pamela, why? Why did you do that?" Oscar asked, saddened by the news.

"I did what was best for the children. I got good money, and it will be enough to go back home and buy a house in Denton. I can go back to work as a seamstress and—"

"Have you signed the land over?" Oscar asked.

"Not yet, why?"

"I'll buy it from you and I'll pay you more," Oscar said.

"I...um, he agreed to pay a lot for it. I don't think you have that sort of money," Pamela said.

"How much?" he asked.

"Three hundred and fifteen and it's yours," she said.

"I'll buy it," he said.

Flabbergasted, she asked, "This will cause you more problems than it's worth, you know that?"

"I'm aware," he said. He decided not to tell her about the contract on their heads nor about Abigail and Grady. He was already planning on going to war with the Hartfords, why not do what he wanted no matter how upset it made them.

PERRY, OKLAHOMA TERRITORY

Franklin arrived at the land office and handed the clerk the document he'd drafted.

"Good day, sir. What, may I ask, is this?" the clerk asked, unfolding the paper.

"A contract for the Jones parcel west of here,"

Franklin said with a smile.

The clerk read it over, his brow furrowing as he went along. "I'm confused."

"Confused about what?" Franklin asked.

"This parcel was just recently sold," the clerk said.

"It's being sold to us, me and my brother, Franklin and Allister Hartford," Franklin said.

"No, sir, the man who purchased this parcel along with the woman who sold it just left here five minutes ago. I was drafting the new deed just now," the clerk said.

Franklin looked down at the clerk's desk and tore the paper from it. He scanned the page until he found the name he was looking for. *Mr. Oscar Milke.* "That son of a bitch."

"Is there a mistake?" the clerk asked.

Franklin tore the deed into pieces and threw it at the bewildered clerk. "Go to hell." He marched out of the office and looked up and down the street, hoping to see Oscar or Pamela. "She double-crossed us."

Owen walked up. He had gone along with Franklin to protect the cash shipment to town. "You're looking peevish," he said.

"She double-crossed us and sold the parcel to Oscar Milke," Franklin replied.

"Imagine that, lied to by a woman." Owen laughed. "I would say it, but I won't."

"Say what?"

"You hired me to kill these people; all of this other stuff is a waste of time. While I've been babysitting you, I could've been out reconnoitering the Milke property. I'm now easily a day behind on this job, all so your brother could save eighty-five dollars."

Seeing James' office, Franklin beelined for it.

"Where you off to now?" Owen asked, growing more agitated.

"I have business with the gentleman," Franklin replied, stopping just outside James' office.

Owen walked up and waited for Franklin to open the door.

"This is a private meeting," Franklin said.

Looking at the sign above the door, Owen said, "Are you buying some lots in town?"

"I'm conducting some business. Now give me a few minutes," Franklin said then entered the office to find James, like usual, sitting at his desk. "Good day."

James lifted his head and peered over his spectacles. "Is that you, Mr. Hartford?"

"It is. I was in town and wanted to stop by," Franklin said.

"Are you here to finalize the transaction?" James asked.

"No, just making sure you didn't sell the lots I wanted."

Removing his glasses, James leaned back in the squeaky chair and said, "Mr. Hartford, I can assure you that I don't violate contracts or agreements."

"So you haven't sold my lots?"

"No, Mr. Hartford, I haven't sold your lots."

"Good, I can tell you that I will be back to get them before the deadline," Franklin said.

"Okay, and thank you for telling me, though it's not necessary; you'll either be here on the fifteenth or not," James said.

"I'll be here," Franklin assured him.

"Is that your partner?" James asked, pointing at Owen, whose face was plastered against the window and looking in.

Embarrassed, Franklin said, "No, he's just a business associate. Thank you for your time." Franklin tipped his hat and exited the office. He grimaced at Owen and barked, "Don't do that again."

"You said I couldn't come in; you said nothing about looking through the window," Owen joked. "So you're buying some lots in town?"

"That's none of your business," Franklin snapped.

"Touchy subject?" Owen asked, finding Franklin's response curious.

Franklin pulled his pocket watch from his vest and flipped it open. "There's still plenty of daylight left to go do what you need to do."

"Are you sure I can safely leave you alone with all that money?" Owen chuckled.

Pocketing his watch, Franklin sneered. "Are you always like this?"

"Like what?"

"Cantankerous," Franklin replied.

"Not familiar with that word, are you saying I'm an ass?" Owen asked.

"In so many words, yes, I am," Franklin said.

A passerby, overhearing Franklin's outburst, stared at

him.

Catching the man's gaze, Franklin hollered as he placed his right hand on the grip of his Colt, "Are you staring at me, huh?"

The passerby, a young man, quickly tore his eyes off Franklin.

"You're really agitated, aren't you?" Owen asked.

Out of the corner of his eye, Franklin spotted a familiar face. "Wait a minute, is that who I think it is?"

"What?" Owen asked, looking around.

"Do you want to get to work right away?" Franklin asked.

"You mean what I think you mean?" Owen asked.

"Yep," Franklin said, pointing across the street to the blacksmith shop. "The man with the dark hair, the small fella with long arms."

"I see him," Owen said.

"That's Robert McGreeley, and he's one of those damn squatters," Franklin said.

"Is he now?" Owen said, spitting tobacco juice on the walkway.

"Go make yourself a hundred dollars," Franklin said, nudging Owen.

Keeping his eyes on the back of Robert, Owen marched across the street. As he went to pass Robert, he deliberately walked into him. "Hey, watch where you're going."

Robert spun around and said, "I'm sorry, my mistake."

Owen shoved him and said, "It is your mistake."

Robert absorbed the shove and said, "Excuse me, mister. I told you I was sorry. Now why did you have to go do a thing like that?"

Several other men nearby all turned and walked away, fearing they might get pulled into trouble.

Owen pulled his long coat back and touched his pistol. "Say something again."

Holding his hands up defensively, Robert said, "Listen, I didn't mean anything by it. Forgive me for walking into you. I'm just here getting some nails. I don't want any trouble."

"C'mon, show me what you got," Owen said, egging Robert on.

Unwilling to fight, Robert shifted his tone and pleaded to be left alone. "Please, mister, I'm sorry. Just let me go about my day."

Seeing he wasn't going to be able to shoot Robert in the street without it looking like murder, Owen pulled back. "You just watch yourself going forward."

"I will."

Owen went back to a dumbfounded Franklin. "Why didn't you kill him?"

"Timing and he didn't want to fight. Also eyeballs everywhere."

"I just thought I was going to witness something magnificent."

Keeping his eye on Robert, Owen watched until he climbed on his wagon and headed out of town. "You want to watch something magnificent?"

"I do," Franklin said.

"Then get on your horse. We're going for a ride," Owen said.

MCGREELEY HOMESTEAD, NOBLE COUNTY, OKLAHOMA TERRITORY

Franklin and Owen followed Robert at a safe distance all the way until he reached his homestead.

Robert was unaware he'd been followed and rode to his house without a care in the world.

Taking up a covered position, Franklin and Owen watched as Robert unloaded the wagon then stowed it and put the horse in the barn. Whistling as he went, he walked back from the barn and into the house.

"How many are living here?" Owen asked.

"Five including Robert," Franklin answered.

Owen pulled his Schofield pistols and made sure they were fully loaded. When he was done, he holstered them both, turned to Franklin and asked, "Are you ready?"

"Are you going to kill them?"

"I am," Owen said.

"All of them?" Franklin asked, knowing it was a silly question.

"Isn't that the reason I'm here?"

"Yes, it is," Franklin said, thrilled that he'd get to witness Owen in action. "I'm excited to actually see the infamous Butcher of Bloody Creek do his dirty work."

"I'm here to entertain," Owen jested then got up. He mounted his horse and called out to Franklin, "Don't just lie there; you're coming with me. Don't you want to see this up close and personal?"

"You want me to go down there with you?" Franklin asked, surprised he was being invited.

"Yeah, c'mon," Owen said.

Franklin mounted his horse and with a smile asked, "Have you ever raped the women before?"

Owen gave him a perplexed stare and said, "I'm not a deviant, and don't think you can do that around me either."

"I wouldn't think of it," Franklin said.

The two raced down to the house, with Owen leaping from his horse before it could even stop. He drew both pistols, cocked them, and briskly walked to the front door. He kicked the door open, stepped inside, and fired upon the first person he saw, a child, killing him with one round. He turned the other pistol on another target, Robert's wife, while cocking his other pistol and fired at her. The round struck her in the side of the torso.

She yelped and stumbled backwards onto the table.

Robert cried out and went for a shotgun.

Owen spun around, took aim and fired.

The round pierced Robert's sternum and exited his back. He dropped to his knees and fell over dead.

Whimpering from the back room got Owen's attention.

Franklin entered the house just as Owen hurried past him towards the back room, where the children's cries were coming from. Horrified as to what was coming next, Franklin stood frozen.

Owen entered the room to find two younger children crying in the corner. He leveled both pistols and fired.

When the gunfire sounded, Franklin jumped. It was done and in less than a minute. Owen had single-handedly killed the entire McGreeley family.

Holstering the pistols, Owen emerged from the back room and said, "You owe me five hundred dollars."

"That was…"

"Was that thrilling for you?"

"It was…"

"Was it magnificent? That was the word you used in town," Owen sneered.

"I've killed men before, but not like this," Franklin said.

"You look queasy." Owen laughed.

"I, um, this was…" Franklin said as he scanned the blood-covered room. His eyes met the dead stare of the older child.

"Are you still excited?" Owen asked.

"What do we do with the bodies?" Franklin asked.

"Leave them where they lie is what I normally do," Owen replied.

"Maybe we should bury them," Franklin said.

Owen shook his head and exited the house. He climbed onto his horse and said, "You go ahead and bury them. I'll meet you back at the house. And, Frank…"

"Yeah."

"Don't ever doubt my conviction to doing my job," Owen said then rode off.

Franklin didn't reply; he simply watched Owen until he disappeared in the distance.

It was true Franklin had never seen anything like he'd just experienced. And it was also true without a doubt that Owen Blake was a butcher, a pure cold-blooded and calculating killer. Owen's brutality and ruthlessness suddenly made Franklin feel uneasy. How could one trust someone like that? Who was to say he wouldn't turn his sights on him or Allister? What he'd just witnessed was disturbing, but the fact was he was responsible for this carnage too. He'd hired the man, brought him to town, and unleashed him.

Of course, Allister would be thrilled, and it would be a good consolation considering they'd lost the Jones land to Oscar.

After much deliberation, Franklin left the bodies of the McGreeleys lie where they had died, but would dispose of them by burning the house down. He dumped all the lantern oil he could find throughout the house and set the place ablaze.

As he stood watching the flames engulf the house, his thoughts turned towards being done with this entire chapter of his life. He still hadn't come to grips with how he'd tell Allister that he was going to buy two lots in town, but maybe once this was over, he wouldn't care.

His anger in town had prompted this attack, but now that it was over, he regretted it. There was killing and then there was murder; and what Owen had done wasn't just murder, it was barbaric. With his conflicting thoughts and regret plaguing his mind, he mounted his horse and rode back towards home.

NOBLE COUNTY, OKLAHOMA TERRITORY

In the distance Oscar saw a black plume of smoke rising. The plume was so large it had to be a structure fire. Concern gripped him. He lashed his horse until he was racing towards it at full speed. He cleared a small rise and looked down on the charred and blackened remains of Robert's house. Oscar leapt from his horse. "Robert!"

No reply.

"Anyone here? Robert! Candace!" he screamed.

He spotted something in the ruins and walked towards it to discover the top half of a skull sticking out of a pile of ash. He waded through the remains of the house to find more bones. When he was done, he had found five sets of remains, no doubt meaning that the entire McGreeley family had been killed, but the question was had they been murdered, or was this an accident? Immediately he knew the answer had to be murder. An uncontrollable shaking overcame him; his vision narrowed; then nausea soon followed. He dropped to his knees and began to vomit.

His mind spun with visions of Allister and Franklin savagely killing the McGreeleys then setting the house ablaze to cover their grisly crime.

Using his sleeve, he wiped the vomit that clung to his chin and slowly stood. Terror suddenly filled him. If the Hartford brothers were capable of killing Robert and his family without prejudice, they could come for his family too.

He ran to his horse, jumped on and took off, praying that when he arrived home, he wouldn't be greeted by a similar scene.

MILKE HOMESTEAD, NOBLE COUNTY, OKLAHOMA TERRITORY

A frantic Oscar rode up and jumped from his horse. "Agatha!"

Hearing the fear in his voice, Agatha exited the house to find Oscar coming towards her with a look of terror on his face. "He killed them all!"

"Who?" Agatha asked, taking Oscar into her arms and comforting him.

"They burned their house to the ground," Oscar said.

"Who?" she asked again.

"Robert and his family, they're all dead," Oscar answered.

"All of them?" Agatha asked.

"Yes, all of them, including the children," Oscar said.

Grady ran up. "What's going on?"

"They, the Hartford brothers, attacked and killed the McGreeley family," Oscar replied.

"They killed the entire family?" Grady asked.

"Yes, all of them. I found their bodies in their burned-out house," Oscar answered.

"Then we need to prepare because they'll come here," Grady said.

"Yes, we should, but I need to get my family out of here," Oscar said.

Abigail emerged from the shed. She tucked her shirt into her trousers and called out, "What's all the commotion?"

"The Hartford brothers attacked and killed their neighbors. They killed them all, including the wife and children," Grady replied.

Abigail thought about what Grady had just told her. She went back into the shed and came back out with her boots and her gun belt slung over her shoulder.

"Agatha, go gather the children. Pack a few things and head to the Jones homestead. It will be safe there," Oscar ordered.

"Are you sure?" Agatha asked.

"Yes, I'm sure, and take the shotgun with you," Oscar said.

Agatha rushed inside the house.

Abigail walked up and said, "You should go with your family."

"I need to stay here," Oscar said.

"There's no need for that; we're here," Abigail said to Oscar then turned to Grady and asked, "How many men do these brothers have?"

"One, but there could be more," Grady replied.

Abigail thought for a second then said, "We don't wait for them to attack us; we ride out and attack them."

Shocked by her plan, Grady asked, "You want to attack them?"

"Yes," she answered confidently.

"Why?" Grady asked.

"Because it's the last thing they'd expect; we'd have the upper hand. We go just after midnight," Abigail said.

"If you're going to do that, I'm riding with you," Oscar said.

Beads of sweat began to form on Abigail's brow.

"You're sweating," Grady said.

"I'm hot," she replied.

"You don't—" Grady said before being interrupted by her.

"I'm fine. I'll rest some more before we go, but I'm fit enough to do this," Abigail said.

"I'll take my family to the Jones homestead and meet you back here before dusk," Oscar said, walking away to help Agatha before she could protest.

Alone, Grady asked, "Isn't it safer to lie in wait?"

"No, we have no idea when they'll come. By us attacking them, we take control of the situation and aren't reacting to it," she said.

"I won't argue with you. If you say we're attacking them tonight, then I suppose we're attacking," Grady said, relenting to her will.

She patted him on the shoulder and said, "Over time you'll just nod without any complaint, as you'll see I know what I'm doing."

"Pride before the fall," he quipped.

"Not pride, but confidence," she fired back.

"Let's put aside this confidence of yours and get real. Are you capable of riding out tonight?"

"Yes," she said.

"Okay, then tonight we ride," Grady said.

"Good," she said, winking before walking away.

"Where are you going?"

"Wake me up in a few hours," Abagail answered.

"Wait, you said you're ready to go," he hollered.

Not looking back, she replied, "I said I'd be ready tonight, not now."

HARTFORD RANCH, NOBLE COUNTY, OKLAHOMA TERRITORY

Franklin reached for the front door latch, but before he could grab it, the door opened wide and Owen was standing there with a large grin on his face.

"I think I'll give you and your brother some privacy," Owen said, walking out past Franklin.

Confused by the comment, Franklin looked inside to see Allister sitting at the main table, and in front of him was the small chest where they kept their money. Franklin gulped and stepped inside. "Did Owen tell you about the McGreeleys?"

"He did," Allister answered.

"Good, I should tell you about it," Franklin said.

"Close the door behind you and come sit down. We need to talk," Allister said.

Fearful, Franklin did as his brother asked, taking a seat across from him.

"Upon Owen's arrival, he asked that I pay him right away for the killings of the McGreeleys. Now, as you know, you normally handle the money, so I wanted to wait, but he really insisted." Allister shifted in his chair and continued. "I didn't know when you'd return, and he was being quite pain in my ass, so I decided to handle it. I unlock the box to find some of the money missing."

"Are you referring to the money I took to pay off Mrs. Jones? By the way, did Owen tell you what she did?" Franklin asked, hoping to divert the conversation, as he knew where it was going.

"Let's just establish that he told me everything," Allister said.

"She double-crossed us," Franklin sneered.

"It's fine. I'll get that land after Mr. Blake kills them, so I'm not too concerned. As he reminded me, I made the deal with her to save some money; but, alas, it didn't work out," Allister said. He placed both elbows on the table and leaned closer to Franklin. "Brother, I'm going to ask you once and only once. Did you take money out of here?" Allister asked.

The desire to lie was strong, but Allister could spot a lie quicker than anything. Hoping he'd be able to muster a worthy excuse, he blurted out, "I took the money to put a deposit on two lots in town."

Allister's eyes widened. "A deposit for lots? What does that mean?"

"There are two lots in town, very desirable locations, ones where we could build a saloon and gambling hall, even have prostitutes and a hotel. You should see the lots," Franklin answered.

Allister's face began to turn flush as anger swelled in him.

"Just come to town with me. I'll show you," Franklin said.

"You get your ass back on that horse and go get that money back," Allister barked.

"I can't," Franklin said.

"Why not?"

"On account that it's a nonrefundable deposit. He's holding the lots for a week to give me time to…"

"To what? Spit it out," Allister barked.

"Convince you."

Allister slammed his clenched fist against the tabletop and hollered, "How many times have we had this conversation? Huh? You're a damn drunk, Frank. You can't own a saloon; you can't be near booze. The stuff nearly killed you, don't you remember that?"

"Al, this is an opportunity. Just please come into town and see the lots, please," Franklin said.

Allister jumped up and yelled, "Go to town now, and get my money back."

"No."

"What did you just say?" Allister asked.

"No, I won't. That money is mine. I took a part of my share, and a few days from now, I'll take more to go buy them lots. I'm going to build a saloon and gambling hall."

Unable to control his ire, Allister rushed over and snatched Franklin by the collar. "You're not going to defy me. If you won't go willingly, I'll drag your ass to town."

"Get your hands off me," Franklin warned, finding some courage.

"So it's going to be that way, is it?" Allister asked.

"I'm buying those lots and that's that," Franklin said defiantly.

In a fit of anger, Allister shoved Franklin.

Losing his footing, Franklin tumbled to the floor and hit his head against the fireplace.

Not stopping his attack, Allister marched over, took Franklin by the collar, and dragged him outside.

When Owen saw what was happening, he chuckled.

"Just know that I'm doing this for you, little brother," Allister said, dragging a semiconscious Franklin down towards the barn.

"Will you be needing any help?" Owen called out.

"Shut up," Allister fired back.

"I won't do it. I won't be bullied into not buying those lots," Franklin said as he tried to free himself from Allister's grasp.

Stopping, Allister looked down at his brother and roared, "Why? Huh?" He added, "'Cause you'll only kill yourself."

"It's my life. If I want to kill myself, then let me do it!" Franklin hollered.

Those words struck Allister and made him think. Was he doing the right thing? Was he his brother's keeper?

"I left home 'cause Pa was acting like you, telling me what to do and how to live," Franklin said.

Allister released his grip.

Franklin hopped to his feet and dusted himself off.

"Do what you want. Just go, leave," Allister said as

he changed his mind.

"Leave?" Franklin asked, showing confusion at the sudden change in Allister's attitude.

"If you want to kill yourself with booze, go ahead; you're right, it's your life. If you want to live it at the bottom of a bottle, then go ahead," Allister said.

Franklin turned to head back to the house.

"Where are you going?" Allister asked.

"To get my things," Franklin said as he kept walking.

"No, leave now. Take your horse and go," Allister said.

"I'm not leaving without my clothes," Franklin said.

"Owen!" Allister called out.

Looking over, Owen asked, "What?"

"Stop my brother from entering the house," Allister said.

"You didn't hire me to handle domestic situations. You stop him," Owen said as he pinched some tobacco from a pouch and put it in his lower lip.

Franklin entered the house, grabbed some of his personal effects, and reemerged with a bag slung over his shoulder. He sauntered to his horse and tossed the bag over the back.

"It didn't have to be this way, little brother," Allister said.

Not listening to him, Franklin mounted the horse. "To hell with you."

"Don't you dare come back begging once you've drank all your money away," Allister said, acknowledging that Franklin had the money from earlier on him.

Ignoring him, Franklin left the ranch without saying another word to Allister.

With Franklin gone, Allister headed over to Owen. "I suppose you find humor in this?"

"To be honest, I don't. I had a brother, and unfortunately he and I stopped talking after what happened in Bloody Creek. He died a year later. I'm left knowing my brother hated me; it's not a good feeling."

"Am I wrong for letting him go and kill himself?" Allister asked.

"I learned a long time ago that the only person you have control over is yourself. If Frank wants to dive into a bottle and it kills him, that's his choice. It's sad to see that happen, but if you stop or prevent someone from living their lives, they'll only end up resenting you or, worse, hating you."

"How about we go into town and get a few drinks?" Allister asked.

"I'll go with you, but not if you're going there to find Frank and convince him to stay," Owen said.

"No, I'm not. I just want to get away from here for a while," Allister said. "And the drinks are on me."

"I like the sound of that," Owen said.

PERRY, OKLAHOMA TERRITORY

Owen and Allister entered the Blue Bell Saloon, and the first person Allister saw was Franklin, who stood at the bar with a glass of whiskey in his hand.

"You said we didn't come here to start anything,"

Owen said, reminding Allister of his promise.

"I'm not here to do that. I just need a drink," Allister said handing Owen ten dollars to pay for the drinks before walking away to find a table near the back.

Owen made his way to the bar, motioned to the bartender, and waited for him to come up.

Franklin caught sight of Owen and shook his head in displeasure.

"What do ya need?" the bartender asked.

"A bottle and two glasses," Owen said.

The bartender pulled a bottle from behind him and placed two shot glasses next to it. "That'll be five dollars."

Owen flipped a coin onto the bar and said, "Send a bottle to my friend down there." He motioned with his head towards Franklin.

"Sure thing," the bartender said.

Franklin grimaced at Owen, but when the bottle appeared and the bartender told him where it came from, the disgusted look on his face melted away. He waved at Owen and lifted a glass as if toasting him.

Owen nodded, took the bottle and glasses, and headed for the table, weaving around a packed floor of people. "I don't think he's happy to see me," Owen said.

"I don't want to talk about him anymore. Sit down and let's talk about how you're going to finish your business up here."

Taking a seat, Owen filled the glasses and slid one over to Allister, picked his up and said, "To ending your squatter problem."

"I'll toast to that," Allister said, raising his glass.

Owen tossed the entire amount back while Allister took a large sip and set it down.

"Not a drinker, are you?" Owen asked.

"No, Frank's got that covered for the family," Allister replied.

Owen filled his glass again and drank it immediately. Wiping his mouth, he said, "I head out to the Milke place tomorrow. Depending on how it looks, I might be through with this then."

"I hope you are. Then you can be on your way," Allister said.

"Are you not liking my company?" Owen joked.

"The sooner I can get back to work, the better; I've got big things I'm doing with my land," Allister said.

James Reeder entered the saloon, looked around, and spotted Franklin at the bar. He went directly up to him and said, "Fancy meeting you here."

Franklin scoffed and said, "Can't a man get a drink in peace?"

"I apologize, I didn't realize you were upset. I hope it has nothing to do with me," James said.

"Listen, old man, I'll have the rest of the money to you tomorrow; tonight I'd like to just drink alone," Franklin said.

"Then I'll leave you be," James said and moved down a few feet.

Irritated, Franklin snatched the bottle Owen had bought him and exited the bar.

James watched him leave and shrugged his shoulders, confused as to why Franklin was so upset. Getting the bartender's attention, he ordered a beer.

With the beer in hand, he spun around and scanned the saloon, looking for any potential prospects to sell lots to. His eyes stopped when he spotted Allister. He adjusted his bow tie, cleared his throat and walked towards them. Stopping a foot away, he said, "Good evening, gentlemen. My name is James Reeder, and I want to talk to you about an opportunity."

"Go piss off," Allister barked.

"Oh my," James said, shocked by the bristly response.

"Don't just stand there, move along," Allister barked.

"Very well, you have a nice evening," James said.

Recognizing James, Owen asked, "What's the opportunity?"

"Do you really want to know what he's selling? It's probably some potion or elixir," Allister sneered.

"Sir, I can tell you that I don't sell elixirs or other types of apothecary items. I peddle in something that truly holds value and is an asset that will appreciate over time. What I sell is a real investment because it's real estate."

"You sell land?" Owen asked.

"Yes, sir, but not just land, I sell lots in town, and I can tell you that they're one of the most coveted things around. If you'll let me sit down, I'd love to discuss my vision for this town and how your investment in lots will result in a windfall of value for you in the not-so-distant future."

"You sell lots in town?" Allister asked.

"Yes, sir," James said with a broad smile stretched across his face.

"Please do sit down and tell me all about this opportunity," Allister said, pushing out a chair next to him for James to sit down.

CHAPTER SIX

HARTFORD RANCH, NOBLE COUNTY, OKLAHOMA TERRITORY

OCTOBER 12, 1893

Abigail could still feel her illness, but she was determined not to let it stop her from the task at hand, killing the Hartford brothers and Owen Blake.

The eight-mile trek to the Hartford ranch felt like an eternity for her, but she suffered through it without uttering a word of protest.

Their plan was simple. Toss torches through the windows, and when they came running out, gun them down. There wasn't a lot that could go wrong, or so they thought.

Armed with a Winchester rifle, Oscar remained unusually quiet.

Abigail sensed it was his nerves. He wasn't a gunman by any stretch of the imagination, so doing something like this made him feel out of place and on edge. Abigail was fine with someone being anxious; she prayed, though, his nerves wouldn't jeopardize the plan.

Grady was also quiet, again unusual for a man who liked to talk as much as anyone she'd ever met. She asked him midway through the ride if he was fine, and he said he was.

When they arrived, they dismounted their horses and

took up a position a hundred yards away from the house.

"Now what?" Oscar asked.

"It's simple. Grady will take up a position at the back of the house; I'll be in view of the front door. Oscar, as we discussed, you're going to toss the torch through the front window," Abigail replied.

"Now?" Oscar asked.

"After Grady gets into position, then you'll head up," Abigail said.

With a rifle in his hand, Grady said, "Give me five minutes."

Abigail nodded.

Grady sprinted off into the darkness.

"Oscar, I can only imagine you're nervous. It's fine to be that way; I just need to know now if you're capable of doing this or not."

Taking a moment to think, Oscar finally replied, "I'm capable."

"You have the torch and matches?" Abigail asked.

"Right here," Oscar said, holding out his hands for her to see, though it was difficult to really do so with no moon.

"Okay, let's go," Abigail said and began to move closer with Oscar following behind. They cleared half the distance when Abigail whispered, "This is where I stop."

Oscar nervously replied, "Then this is it?"

"Are you okay?" she asked.

"I'll admit I'm scared. I hope that doesn't make me a coward," he answered.

"On the contrary, doing something even though you

are afraid is courage, not cowardice," she said. "Now go. Grady is waiting, and there's not a better time than now."

"Abby?" he said.

"Yes."

"Are we doing the right thing?" he asked.

His question shocked her. "These men want your family dead. All you're doing is acting preemptively. So yes, you're doing the right thing."

Oscar swallowed and said, "Very well." He got up and ran towards the house.

Abigail understood his indecisiveness. So often people talked with bravado but would never be faced with acting on their words or threats. Killing men, even those as bad as the Hartford brothers and Owen, while justified in her eyes, could be seen by some as no different. Killing was killing, they'd say, but Abigail looked at it through the lens of good versus evil. These men were evil, they had already committed horrible acts, and Owen was a notorious murderer. Removing these men was not only right, but required, according to her code.

Oscar reached the house. He pressed his back against the rough siding next to the window. He peered in but saw nothing except a table, chairs and a cot, all illuminated by the dim glow of burning embers in the fireplace. *Are they even here?* he asked himself, surprised that he hadn't seen anyone in the cot. Putting his doubts aside, he struck the first match but dropped it on the ground. "Damn it," he muttered under his breath. Taking another match in his trembling hands, he scraped it against the hard sole of his boot. The match flamed to life. He stared at it for a brief second then touched the torch with it. Soaked with lantern oil, the torch lit easily. Taking a deep breath, he said a quick prayer that the plan would work, then, not wasting any more time, smashed the window with his elbow and tossed in the torch.

It only took seconds for the room to become fully engulfed in flames.

He stepped away from the house, and as he slowly moved back, he found himself mesmerized by the flickering flames.

Soon the entire house was ablaze.

From her position, Abigail could see Oscar, but what was missing was any screams or signs of life inside the house.

More time elapsed, but no one cried out, nor did they seek to escape.

Abigail grunted. She knew now without a doubt the house was empty.

"They're not there, they're not there!" Oscar cried out as he ran up to her.

"I know," Abigail replied, getting to her feet.

Grady appeared and repeated almost word for word what Oscar had said.

"We need to fall back to your house and expect a reprisal for this," Abigail said.

"I need to ride to the Jones house and check on my family," Oscar said.

"Agreed. You go; we'll head back to your place," Abigail said.

Oscar sprinted away.

"Now what?" Grady asked.

"Now we wait for them to attack us, unless you have a better idea," she replied.

"Where could they be?" he asked.

"I don't know. I just hope we don't arrive at Oscar's house and find it in this condition," Abigail said.

PERRY, OKLAHOMA TERRITORY

As James escorted Allister and Owen to his office, he wouldn't stop rambling on about the lots and the opportunities Allister would have when he acquired them. "My friend, I will wager that in a year's time you'll be thanking me. Yep, I would definitely put money on that. What you're about to do will change your life, and for the better."

Arriving, James fiddled with a set of keys until he unlocked the front door. He pushed it open, stepped inside, and lit a lantern. The small office filled with light. "Come on inside, gentlemen."

Allister and Owen did as requested.

Owen closed the door and pulled down the blind.

"That wasn't necessary." James laughed as he dug through a side drawer of his desk and pulled out a plat map of town. "Let me show you what I have for sale."

"Are you selling lots to Franklin Hartford?" Allister asked.

Shocked to hear the name, James looked up and recoiled when he saw he was looking down the barrel of

Allister's Remington revolver. "Oh dear."

"Answer me," Allister barked.

Owen leaned against the wall, took a pouch of chewing tobacco out of his pocket, and pinched a little to shove behind his lower lip. He enjoyed moments like this, specifically how someone like James would emotionally handle the knowledge that soon he might be dead.

"I-I, ah..." James stuttered in fear, his arms raised high. "Don't shoot me."

"Did you sell lots to Franklin Hartford?" Allister asked again.

"I haven't sold him anything. He, he, um, he made a deposit is all. I haven't sold him anything," James answered.

"I'm his brother, his older brother, and have been for many years his advisor on such dealings," Allister said.

"Do you not approve of the sale?" James asked.

"No, I don't," Allister said as he thumbed the hammer back on the pistol.

Seeing the cylinder rotate and the hammer fall back, James' fear grew. "Do you not want me to sell him those lots?"

"No, I want you to give him his money back and tell him the lots are no longer for sale," Allister said.

"Oh boy, Frank is going to be pissed." Owen laughed.

"No one asked for your opinion," Allister said.

"I-I-I will do that. He said he was coming by tomorrow. I'll tell him first thing that the lots are not for sale, and I'll refund him the money," James said.

"Can I trust you'll do that?" Allister asked.

"Yes, yes, you can," James stammered.

"If I hear you haven't, I'll come back and put an end to you. Do you understand?" Allister asked.

"Yes, sir, I'll do that. I'll tell him, and I do understand, completely," James said, his voice cracking.

"Good," Allister said as he thumbed the hammer back up. He cocked his head, gave James a crooked smile, then smacked him in the face with the butt of the pistol grip.

James fell back into his chair. He grabbed his face and cried out in pain.

"When you look in the mirror, you'll remember me and remember what you told me," Allister said.

"I won't sell him any lots," James moaned.

"Good, we understand each other," Allister said. He turned to Owen and continued, "Let's leave Mr. Reeder to his business."

"A shame, I was hoping you'd kill him," Owen said.

"I will if he doesn't do what I ask," Allister said.

Both men left the office.

MILKE HOMESTEAD, NOBLE COUNTY, OKLAHOMA TERRITORY

Abigail was happy to see Oscar's house was untouched, but she then wondered if Oscar and his family were fine. "Do you know where this Jones house is?"

"No," Grady said as he dug through the small pantry inside the house.

Sitting at the table, Abigail put her head in her hands and sighed. "Ugh, I'm starting to feel like hell again."

"Best you go lie down," Grady said. He found some dried beef and rejoiced. "Yes, food." He pulled it out and threw it on the table. "Hungry?"

Seeing the meat, Abigail shook her head. "No, you help yourself to all of it."

"What should we do next?" Grady said, taking a seat across from her. He picked through the meat and found a piece to his liking.

"We wait here until Oscar comes back, but I really don't know what to do but sit tight and wait for them to ride in," Abigail replied.

"Once they find their home destroyed, they'll come here, I don't doubt that," Grady said, chewing on a piece of meat.

"Then we'll need to be ready," Abigail said.

"We will be, but what I want to know is, can we go find a job that pays money next?" Grady asked.

"Is that all you think about?" Abigail asked.

"Money is not the only thing, it's not even number one, but it's up there," Grady answered.

"We will go find a job and get you paid," she said.

"I'll have you know, the money is so I can send it back to Kentucky," Grady explained.

Lifting her head and looking at him, she asked, "Who's in Kentucky?"

"My mother is," he replied.

"And your father?" she asked.

"Dead some five years now. She needs it to live, so I

have it wired to her every month," Grady said.

Feeling bad about her earlier tone, she said, "Let's get through this and we'll score ourselves a new job, one that pays good. I'll even give you a portion of my cut because I know you don't really want to do this."

"That's not necessary. I just need to make some money and soon," he said.

"I never thought you might need the money for something like that," she said.

Seeing the dark circles under her eyes and the weariness in her face, he said, "You need to go sleep. I'll take watch until dawn."

"I'll take you up on that offer," she said, getting to her feet. She headed to the door but stopped, putting her hand on his shoulder. "You're a good man, Grady; you really are."

"Don't tell anyone, okay; I don't want to ruin my bad name," he joked.

Making a hand gesture over her chest, she said, "Cross my heart, your secret is safe with me."

"Good night, Abby," he said.

"Good night, Grady."

HARTFORD RANCH, NOBLE COUNTY, OKLAHOMA TERRITORY

Seeing the smoldering remains of his house sent Allister into a blind rage. He threw whatever he could get his hands on and cursed until the anger finally subsided. Now calm, he began to pace back and forth, his mind spinning as to who might have done this. He had his suspicions that it was Oscar, but he also suspected his brother. He had seen Franklin leave the saloon before he started talking to James and wondered if he'd ridden all the way back and set the house on fire. Could he have done something like this? Would he?

"It has to be those squatters," Owen said.

"But it could also be my brother. He's been known to act impulsively when he's drunk," Allister said.

"Frank would do something like this?" Owen asked.

"He is capable, but I think you're right, it was Oscar. He came here to attack us for what happened to the McGreeleys," Allister said but still couldn't get the thought of Franklin out of his mind.

"Then there's only one thing to do right now, and that's to ride there and kill them all," Owen said.

"We will, but not right now, they'll be expecting us. We need to think about this, fight back in a way they won't be expecting us to," Allister said as he paced in front of the remains of his house.

"And that is?" Owen asked.

"I don't have the answer yet, but any ideas from you would be welcome," Allister replied.

"I say we ride there now and kill them. It's just him and his family; you and me together can finish this."

"He's gonna be waiting for us. We might not make it within a hundred feet," Allister said.

"When is he not going to be waiting for us?" Owen asked.

Still pacing and deep in thought, Allister held out his

hand and said, "Let me think."

Owen shook his head out of frustration.

Thinking out loud, Allister said, "If I were Oscar and I planned on coming to kill me, I'd probably put my family somewhere safe, somewhere that wasn't home. Where would that be?"

"Town?" Owen asked.

"No, he took his family to the Jones homestead. He has to assume we're going to come for him, so he would have taken the precautionary step of taking them there. He would feel that's a safe place."

"Then we ride there and kill his family," Owen said.

"No, we ride there and take his family hostage," Allister said.

"I don't get paid for taking people hostage," Owen reminded him.

"I'll pay you no matter what. If we kill them, Oscar will come after us. If we take them, we get him to sign over both parcels in exchange for his family. We get him to go away without having to fire another shot," Allister said.

"You'll pay me the money per head regardless?" Owen asked.

"Yes, I'll pay you," Allister said.

Owen walked towards his horse. "Then let's go rustle up his family."

JONES HOMESTEAD, NOBLE COUNTY, OKLAHOMA TERRITORY

Allister was more determined than ever to win this conflict with Oscar. When they arrived just outside the old Jones house, the sun was beginning to make its presence known to the east. The much-needed light was helpful, especially when they saw Oscar leaving the house and going to his horse.

"Where do you suppose he's going?" Owen asked, peering through binoculars.

"Back to his house, I'd reckon," Allister said, also using a set of binoculars.

"Let me take him now. I can get a clean shot and end this all. We're just wasting time with kidnapping and ransom; I can end this now," Owen said.

Allister didn't like changing plans, but Owen was right; if he could just kill Oscar now, this entire episode would be over. "Do it."

Owen picked up his Winchester Model 73, lifted the long-range rear sight aperture, and adjusted it for the estimated distance. He firmly got behind the rifle, placing the butt of the rear stock into the pocket of his shoulder, made positive contact with his cheek, and took aim through the peep sight. He placed his index finger on the trigger and began to apply pressure.

Unbeknownst to Oscar, the sights of a .44-40-caliber rifle were pointed at his back. One round was all it would take to end his life.

The door of the house opened up and out came

Thomas. "Pa, wait up."

Oscar moved away from the horse and over to see Thomas.

"Damn," Owen grumbled, taking aim again on Oscar.

"What is it?" Oscar asked.

"Can I come with you, please?" Thomas asked.

"No, son, I need you here to watch over your mother and siblings. You're the man of the house with me away."

"But, Pa, I can be of help against those Hartford brothers," Thomas groaned.

"Just do as I ask," Oscar said, turning away and quickly walking back to his horse.

Again, Owen's shot was disrupted. But instead of pivoting all the way back, he turned ever so slightly and put his sights on Thomas' chest.

"Pa, when are you ever going to let me help out?" Thomas complained.

"Thomas, you are helping out," Oscar said, fastening the saddle tight on the horse.

"What are you waiting for?" Allister asked.

"Sssh," Owen said, starting to squeeze the trigger.

Oscar hopped on the horse then noticed he hadn't untied him. "Thomas, can you untie the horse?"

Moving to do what he was asked, Thomas walked over and untied the horse from the post.

Frustrated once more, Owen decided against taking the harder shot at the boy and put his sights back on Oscar, this time his chest, and applied pressure to the trigger.

"What on earth are you waiting for?" Allister growled.

Ignoring Allister, Owen focused his breathing and kept squeezing until the rifle fired, surprising him. He followed through with the shot for a couple of seconds, then worked the lever action to load another round.

The round traveled the two hundred and sixty yards and struck Oscar in his stomach. He bent over and toppled from the horse.

"Pa!" Thomas cried out.

The front door of the house opened, and out came a screaming Agatha.

"Time to go to work," Owen said, taking aim on Agatha as she knelt next to Oscar, her hand over the wound in his gut. After seeing where his first shot went, he aimed a little higher and squeezed off another round. The round hit Agatha in the neck and almost severed her head from her body. She fell to her side, dead.

"No!" Oscar wailed, crawling towards her.

"Ma!" Thomas screamed, dropping to his knees and cradling her barely attached head in his lap.

The younger children stepped out of the house and stared in terror at the scene before them.

"Get back inside, go, get back inside!" Oscar screamed at the younger ones. "Thomas, you too, go!" he pleaded.

Owen cycled the Winchester, placed his sights on Thomas, and began to squeeze.

"She's dead, Pa, she's dead!" Thomas wailed.

"Thomas, go, get inside the house!" Oscar hollered.

"No, I'm going to go get Abigail and Grady. They can help us!" he cried out, jumping to his feet just as Owen's rifle fired again. The round just missed him.

"Then go, ride as fast as you can!" Oscar screamed.

Thomas leapt onto the horse, kicked the sides of it hard, and sprinted away.

"Stop the boy, hurry!" Allister barked.

Owen aimed and fired, but his shot missed. He cycled the lever action again and quickly fired, but once more his aim was off.

Oscar crawled his way to the house and managed to get inside, closing the door behind him.

Allister got to his feet and barked, "C'mon, let's go finish him."

Aggravated at not delivering a lethal shot to Oscar, Owen stood and grunted, "I'll get him, damn it, I will."

The two men ran to their horses, climbed on, and made for the house, determined to finish Oscar off.

Inside the house, Oscar crawled to the fireplace, where his shotgun was, a trail of blood behind him.

William and Elizabeth ran up to him crying, their little cheeks flush and their eyes red. "Pa, Pa!"

With his hand covered in blood, he reached up and touched Elizabeth's face. "I need you to look outside for me. See if anyone is coming."

"I'm scared," she wailed, her tiny hand clinging to his arm.

"William, can you do it for your sister, please?" Oscar said as he shifted on the floor, sending pain through his body.

Not hesitating, William went to the closest window and peered out. In the distance he spotted a cloud of dust. "I see someone coming, Pa. I can't make out how many though."

"How far away are they? Can you tell?" Oscar asked.

"They're just coming down the bluff near the big rock," William replied. The big rock he was referring to was approximately two hundred yards away.

"Good, now go to the back window," Oscar said.

William did as he was told. "I don't see anything, Pa."

"Good, now come here, hurry," Oscar said.

William came and knelt next to him.

"I need you to take your sister and make a run for it. Head out the back window, go straight out, and take cover in the dry creek bed. You know the one, you two play in it all the time."

William nodded while Elizabeth kept sobbing.

"I need you to go now, don't hesitate, and, William, take my pistol with you. I taught you how to use it. Do you remember?"

"Yes, Pa, I do," William said.

"Good boy," Oscar said, tears welling up in his eyes.

"But what about you?" William asked.

"Don't worry about me. Now go, hurry, run as fast as you can," Oscar insisted, pushing them away and handing William the shotgun.

Taking Elizabeth's hand, William walked her to the window, pushed it open, and helped her climb out. He handed her the pistol; then he went through it. Before turning and racing away, he gave Oscar one last look and said, "Love you, Pa."

"I love you too. Now go, hurry!" Oscar said.

The young children did as they were told and sprinted away.

Oscar knew his time was short, but he wasn't going to go out without a fight. He dragged himself across the floor to the front window, got to his knees, and peered out through the smudged windows. The cloud of dust was closer; however, they were far enough away for him to set up a trap. He spotted the shed and got an idea that would be better than using the shotgun. Using all the strength he could muster, he lifted himself up and stood. Vertigo began to wash over him, but he steadied himself enough to move back to the fireplace. There he found a box of matches. He snatched them and staggered to the door and went outside. The first thing his eyes cast down on was Agatha's dead body lying in a large pool of blood. "I'm so sorry, my love," he said. Allister and Owen were close enough now that he could hear the horses galloping. Finding the will and determination, he made for the shed, which sat forty feet away. Putting one foot in front of the other, he began his march.

The distance, though relatively short, felt like it could have been a mile to him; but he made it and with time to spare. He tossed open the latch and threw the door open. The sunlight illuminated the contents of the small space, and tucked in the corner he found what he was looking for. A large smile stretched across his face as he closed the door and locked himself inside.

Allister and Owen both saw Oscar head to the shed, and made that their final destination.

When they arrived, Owen was the first to dismount. He pulled his rifle from the scabbard, cocked the hammer on the Winchester, as a round was already chambered, aimed and fired into the shed. He cycled the rifle and fired again. "I know you're in there!"

Allister's target wasn't the shed. He went for the house to find the other children he'd last seen running inside. "Come on out, children. I won't hurt you!" he lied.

Owen continued firing into the shed until he emptied his rifle. He tossed it aside, pulled one of his Smiths, and advanced on the front door. "Time to finally finish you off."

Cautiously making his way inside the house, Allister found it was empty. Angered by this revelation, he stepped outside and saw Owen reaching for the door of the shed.

Inside the shed, Oscar had been hit twice by the rifle fire but was still able to do what he came there for: light a stick of dynamite. The fuse had burned down to within a quarter inch when the door opened, and there stood Owen, pistol in hand and devilish grin on his face. Not seeing Allister, Oscar groaned his last breath at not killing his nemesis.

When Owen cast his gaze on Oscar then saw the dynamite, he turned as swiftly as he could to escape the blast, but it was too late.

The dynamite exploded, which set the entire box of

it off.

The concussion from the blast was so intense that Allister was thrown back inside the house and left unconscious.

PERRY, OKLAHOMA TERRITORY

Franklin left the boardinghouse and headed straight for James Reeder's office. Today he'd make it official. With each step he took, his pride swelled, and the knowledge that soon he'd be his own man filled him with joy.

To every person he saw along his way, he tipped his hat and gave salutations and greetings. He leapt onto the walkway, grabbed the doorknob of James' office door and turned it to find it locked. He pulled out his pocket watch to find it was late enough for James to be open. Stepping to the side, he peered through the glass and saw James sitting at his desk.

Tapping on the window, Franklin called out, "Open up."

James ignored him.

Franklin tapped harder.

"Go away!" James barked.

"I've got the money. I want to complete the transaction," Franklin hollered through the glass.

"The lots aren't for sale anymore!" James replied, still hiding his face.

"What!"

"Go away."

Franklin walked back to the door and jiggled the

knob. "Open the damn door!"

Fearful but knowing Franklin wouldn't easily go away, James reluctantly got up and unlocked the door.

Stepping inside, Franklin barked, "What do you mean the lots aren't for sale anymore?"

Walking back to his desk to get some distance in between him and Franklin, James replied, "They're not, I'm sorry." He reached into his desk, pulled out a single hundred-dollar bill and handed it to Franklin. "Here's your deposit back."

Finally seeing his badly bruised face, Franklin asked, "What happened to you?" A second after he asked, he knew the answer. "Wait, it was my brother, wasn't it?"

"Just take your money and go, leave," James snapped.

"No, I won't allow this to happen. You're going to sell me those lots or…"

"Or you're going to kill me too?" James snarked.

"He threatened you, is that what he did?" Franklin asked.

"Listen, you and your brother need to hash things out, but until I know for sure my life is not in jeopardy, those lots are not for sale to you. Now please leave, Mr. Hartford."

"No, you're going to sell me those lots, you hear me?"

"No, I am not. Now please leave. I have business to attend to," James said, his eyes carefully watching Franklin's every move.

Understanding the fear James was feeling, Franklin

knew he had to find a way to make James feel secure enough to sell him the lots. "What if my brother wasn't a problem?"

"Mr. Hartford, I'm not sure what you can do. Your brother was adamant, and look what he did to my face," James said.

"I'll fix this. Don't sell those lots," Franklin said.

"I can't hold the lots, I'm sorry," James said.

Using the one negotiating tactic he knew, Franklin drew his pistol, cocked it and said, "You're going to hold onto that hundred and not sell the lots. If I return and find you've sold them, you won't have to worry about my brother."

James sighed loudly and said, "I won't sell them, but you do know the situation I'm in, don't you?"

"I'll handle this once and for all," Franklin said then left the office.

MILKE HOMESTEAD, NOBLE COUNTY, OKLAHOMA TERRITORY

Thomas rode in screaming, "Abigail, Grady, help!"

Having been awake to take her shift so Grady could sleep, Abigail sat up from her position perched just inside the house near the window and came out of the house.

Not waiting for his horse to even stop, Thomas jumped from the back of the horse, tumbled to the ground hard and rolled.

Abigail went to him. "Thomas, what's wrong?"

"My ma, she's dead, and Pa, he's been shot!"

Thomas replied before bursting into tears.

"Grady, get up, get your ass up now!" Abigail hollered.

Having already heard the commotion, Grady exited the shed with his gun belt hung over his shoulder and his rifle in his hand. "I heard you ride in."

"Saddle up the horses. We're riding to finish this," Abigail said.

Thomas wrapped his arms around her and sobbed.

Tenderly touching his head, she softly said, "I need you to be strong. Can you do that?"

He nodded.

"Can you lead us to the Jones place?" she asked.

"Yes."

"How far away is it?"

"Forty minutes if we ride hard," he said.

"We'll do that. Now tell me, where's your brother and sister?" Abigail asked, hoping his answer wasn't dreadful.

"They were still there, that's all I know," he replied, his words muffled in her shirt.

"We'll rescue them," she said, stopping herself from saying she'd promise to do so.

Grady walked up holding the reins of his horse and Cloud. "Do we have a plan?"

"Thomas, how many men were there?" Abigail asked, ignoring Grady's question.

"Two, I think. I think I saw two," Thomas answered.

"Good, now get back on your horse and lead us there," she said.

Thomas let go and went back to his horse.

"You didn't answer my question. What's the plan?" Grady asked.

She looked up at the midmorning sun and said, "Looks like it's going to be a beautiful day."

"That's not an answer," Grady groaned.

"Before I ever do something where I might be killed, I'm sure to always appreciate the world around me because it could be my last time seeing it."

"Can I assume we're just riding in guns blazing?" he asked, knowing her modus operandi.

Taking Cloud's reins, she hopped on his back, pulled back and replied, "It's what I do."

"Is that your answer for everything?" he asked, climbing onto his horse.

"I've gotten this far doing it that way." She grinned.

"Then it's guns blazing, I guess," Grady said.

JONES HOMESTEAD, NOBLE COUNTY, OKLAHOMA TERRITORY

Allister opened his eyes. Above him he saw the ceiling and support beams of the house. He moved his right arm, then his left. Sitting up, he looked around and saw he was lying in the middle of the room. He recalled the explosion but not what had happened immediately after it. Being that he was where he was, he had to assume he had been blown back inside the house and knocked out from the blast.

Feeling something warm and wet near his left ear, he

reached up and touched it. He brought his finger out so he could see it and saw it was covered in blood. This could only mean he'd blown his eardrums, hence why his head was ringing.

Outside, he saw the crater left by the explosion. Its sheer size told him that there was no way Owen survived the blast.

Footfalls sounded from outside.

Allister reached for his sidearm but found his holster empty. He looked around and saw his gun lying a foot away. Not knowing who was coming, he reached out and grabbed it.

"Put the pistol down, big brother," Franklin ordered.

Allister turned his head slowly and saw Franklin towering in the doorway, the muzzle of a pistol pointed at him. "Isn't this something, baby brother?"

"I was coming to speak to you when I saw the plume of smoke. I decided to come investigate, and lo and behold, I find you," Franklin said.

"How about you help your big brother up?" Allister said, holding out his left hand.

"What happened?" Franklin asked.

Allister chuckled and replied, "I underestimated Mr. Milke's resolve, that's what that is."

"Where's Owen?" Franklin asked.

"He's out there," Allister answered.

"Where?"

"A bit over there and some over there," Allister joked. "Now help me up."

"You went and talked to Mr. Reeder last night,"

Franklin said.

"I did, but you know it's for your own good," Allister said.

"You're going to go back and tell him I'm buying those lots," Franklin sneered.

"How about we talk about this after you help me up?" Allister asked. "And can you please point that somewhere else?"

"Take your hand off yours and I'll think about lowering mine," Franklin said.

Allister looked back towards his pistol. He brought his right hand back and held both up. "Now will you help me up?"

"Can I trust you?" Franklin asked.

"We might disagree and even fight, but you're still my brother, my blood; now help me up," Allister said.

Franklin decocked his pistol and holstered it. He took Allister's left hand into his and pulled him up.

Standing eye to eye and a foot apart, Allister grinned and said, "Thank you, brother."

"Now saddle up. We're riding into town. You need to tell Mr. Reeder you're not going to kill him."

Wiping the thick dust from his trousers, Allister said, "I'm not going to do that."

"Yes, you are," Franklin said.

"Frank, you need me looking after you. If I just let you do what you want, you'll be dead within six months. I couldn't live with myself if that happened."

"Damn it, Al, you're going into town with me now or..."

Shoving Franklin aside, Allister took a step but was stopped in his tracks when he heard the distinct cocking of a pistol. "Now, little brother, did you just pull your pistol on me again?"

"Get on your horse now," Franklin ordered, his pistol pointed at Allister's back.

"Frank, we're almost done here. All we need to do is track down the Milke children and this chapter in our lives is over. Now put down the pistol," Allister said, slowly turning around to face Franklin and the pistol, which was inches from him.

"No, you're coming with me into town; now move," Franklin crowed.

Out of patience, Allister stepped to the side quickly and reached for the pistol with both hands. His action, while swift, wasn't fast enough.

Franklin pulled the trigger. A round struck Allister through the fleshy part of his side.

All Allister could do was charge Franklin and he did. Wrapping both his arms around Franklin's waist, he tackled him.

Both men struck the hard ground with a thud, with Allister landing on top of Franklin.

With his breath knocked out of him, Franklin gasped for air.

Having the advantage, Allister pulled out his sheath knife and held it point down against his chest and said, "Give up, little brother."

Franklin took in a deep and labored breath. "Never."

Allister pressed the blade down, the point

penetrating the clothes and just the superficial layer of the skin. "Give up."

"You'll have to kill me," Franklin spat.

"I'll do it, don't doubt me," Allister said, pressing harder.

Franklin grasped for anything to fight back with and found his pistol lying next to him. He took it in his hand, cocked it, placed the muzzle against Allister's side, and pulled the trigger.

Allister yelped in pain for an instant then turned it into anger. Using all his strength, he pressed the knife farther into Franklin's chest until it reached the hilt.

Franklin's eyes widened as he stared into Allister's. He gagged then coughed up thick red blood. His body began to shake uncontrollably until it stopped abruptly.

Stunned by what he had done, Allister stared at Franklin's lifeless face. "Frank?"

There would be no reply, for Franklin was dead.

"Frank?" Allister asked again, praying he'd give him an answer.

Allister rolled off Franklin's body and onto his back. He watched the pillowy clouds float by as he thought about his life with Franklin as boys. Tears streamed down the sides of his face. He'd killed his only kin, his blood, and for what?

Galloping horses could be heard in the distance.

Allister touched his side and looked at his hand. It was covered in blood. The gunshot to his side wasn't fatal, but if not taken care of, it would fester. However, someone was coming, and he was sure they were coming for him. Like Oscar before him, he crawled his way back into the house and closed the door. Looking around the room, he took his pistol in his hand; then he spotted a twelve-gauge double-barreled hammer-fire coach shotgun. He crawled to it, found it was loaded, and set himself in the corner of the room and waited.

***

"Whoa, let's stop here," Abigail said, pulling back on Cloud's reins.

Thomas and Grady followed suit.

Grady came to a stop and took out his binoculars. Through the grimy glass he scanned the house and surrounding area.

"This is where you stay," Abigail said to Thomas.

"But I can help, please," Thomas said.

"Not a chance, but what you can do is provide us cover. Are you good with a rifle?" she asked.

"I can shoot bottles at fifty feet," Thomas said.

"Perfect," she said, snatching her rifle from the scabbard and handing it to him. "You're familiar with a lever action, right?"

"Yes, ma'am," Thomas answered, taking the rifle.

"Good, take up a position here and cover us," Abigail said. Turning to Grady, she said, "What do you see?"

"That plume is coming from a huge crater. Something clearly blew up there. I do see a body, oh wait, two bodies near the front door; I can't make out who they are."

"Any movement at all?" she asked.

"Nothing," Grady replied, stowing the binoculars in a pocket of his saddlebag.

Abigail removed her Colt, cocked it and said, "Let's go investigate." She jabbed the sides of Cloud, who responded by sprinting away.

"Watch our backs, kid," Grady said and took off after Abigail.

The two rode up and dismounted near the west side of the house.

"I'll go this way; you go that way," Abigail, said motioning that she'd go around to the front door while he walked around back.

Grady nodded.

Abigail pressed up against the rough siding and walked slowly to the corner. In front of her was the smoldering crater; scattered around it for two hundred feet was debris of all sorts. She peeked her head around the corner and saw the two bodies. One was Agatha and the second was a man she'd never seen before.

Grady, walking along the back, came up to the window and peered in but couldn't see anyone inside from his vantage point, so he continued on.

Feeling she was safe to move, Abigail stepped out from the cover of the house and advanced on the front door. She halted her advance at the front window and snapped a peek inside but couldn't make out much due to the sparsely lit space. With her confidence rising, she went past the window and to the front door, stepping over Agatha's and Franklin's bodies.

Grady emerged from the other side and said, "All clear."

She pointed at the front door and waved him over.

He jogged up next to her and said, "Step aside."

"No, I'm doing it," she said.

He wanted to debate her but let it go.

She stepped back, lifted her leg, and kicked as hard as she could. The door burst in, and with it came the light of day.

Hidden in the shadows near the fireplace, Allister sat, both hammers of the shotgun cocked and the muzzles both pointing directly at Abigail.

Catching a glimpse of Allister hiding, Grady grabbed Abigail's left arm to pull her away.

Allister pulled both triggers and unleashed two barrels of double-aught buck in her direction.

Grady's quick reaction saved her from the brunt of the blast, but her right arm was struck, causing significant damage.

Dazed, Abigail heard her pistol fall to the ground. She looked at it then at her arm, which was dangling. She tried to move her arm but couldn't; then like a wave crashing on her, a darkness came sweeping in. "Grady…" she muttered before dropping to her knees and passing out.

Grady caught her and let her limp body down on the ground gingerly. He wanted to examine her, but there wasn't any time. Someone was in the house and they were determined to kill them.

With the shotgun empty, Allister tossed it aside, took his pistol and cocked it. "Come on, you son of a bitch!"

Grady picked Abigail up off the ground and carried her a safe distance away. How was he going to draw the man out? Like they had done the night before, he'd use fire. Seeing the small barn, he ran for it and found a lantern filled with oil and a match. He lit the lantern, walked up close to the front door, and tossed it in.

The lantern exploded and instantly turned the insides of the house into an inferno.

Allister got to his feet, but the loss of blood was making it hard for him. He staggered to the front door, his pistol out in front of him. He fired two shots outside, then emerged waving the pistol around, hoping he'd spot his aggressor.

Lying in wait, Grady aimed and fired, striking Allister in the right shoulder.

Allister flinched and dropped the pistol.

Grady cocked the pistol, stepped out from his covered position, and fired again, this round striking Allister in the upper chest.

The well-placed shot sent Allister reeling backwards. He landed on his back and gasped.

Not stopping his assault, Grady cocked and fired two more times, both hitting Allister in the upper abdomen.

Coughing up blood, Allister cried out, "Damn you, damn you all to hell."

Using one final shot, Grady cocked his pistol, took aim and said, "You're the only one going to hell." He pulled the trigger.

With Allister dead, Grady went to Abigail's side. He ripped opened her shirt to find that the wound to her arm was catastrophic. "I'm going to get you fixed up, you hear me?" He whistled loudly and hollered for Thomas. "Get down here!" Tending to Abigail again, he wrapped her arm and said over and over, "You're going to be alright. I'm going to take care of you."

CHAPTER SEVEN

PERRY, OKLAHOMA TERRITORY

OCTOBER 14, 1893

Grady emerged from the back bedroom of the boardinghouse, a sour look on his face. In the living room, he found Thomas, William and Elizabeth sitting quietly, their hands resting on their laps.

"How is she?" Thomas asked.

"Her arm is looking bad. I'm going to take her south, to Dallas. I received a telegram today requesting I do that," he said, taking a seat next to them. "The question is what will happen to you."

"I'll be fourteen this winter. I'm more than capable—"

Stopping Thomas before he could finish, Grady said, "No one doubts you, but you have to also think about William and Elizabeth."

"I am thinking of them," Thomas said.

"I've gotten Mr. Reeder to agree to pay a fair amount for the land. This will be more than enough to get you back to Ohio so you can live with your aunt and uncle, plus to save for whatever else you want to do later in life."

"It wasn't Pa's wishes to go back—"

"Son, your ma and pa are gone. We buried your ma yesterday and, well, your time here is over. I'll ride with you as far as the train station and see you off; then I'm taking Ms. Abigail south so she can get the best treatment available to her."

"Will she die?" Elizabeth asked.

Always one to answer honestly, Grady said, "I don't know, but I'm going to do my best to make sure she doesn't."

A knock sounded at the front door of the boardinghouse.

The host, an elderly woman, answered it. "May I help you?"

"My name is Mr. Reeder. I'm here to meet a Mr. Grady."

"Come on in," the woman said.

James entered the house and saw Grady. "Mr. Grady." He looked at the children and continued. "I presume these are the children?"

"They are. Now can you assure me you'll give them the best deal for their land?" Grady asked.

"Oh, the very best. I usually don't deal in land outside town, but for you, I'll make that exception."

"Fair enough, thank you," Grady said.

The two worked out a deal and sealed it with Thomas' signature. James handed him a small envelope of cash and said his goodbyes.

"Now what?" Thomas said.

"We wait until tomorrow; then we ride for the train station. Why don't you get a good night's sleep."

The children got up and left the room.

Grady went back to the bedroom and found Abigail

restless, her head tossing back and forth. Over and over, she kept repeating, "Madeleine, must see her, must get to Dallas." He went and sat on the edge of the bed, took her left hand in his and said, "You're going to see her soon, I promise."

She opened her glassy eyes and said, "Get me home, please."

"I am, I swear it."

EPILOGUE

DALLAS, TEXAS

OCTOBER 25, 1893

Madeleine walked into the room even though she was told not to. She couldn't resist. After being told so many times not to see her, she had to. The room was dark, so she walked to the window and opened the drapes slightly. It was enough for the sun to beam through and chase the darkness away.

The warm rays hit Abigail's face.

Upon seeing her, Madeleine made her way to the bedside and sat. She looked down on Abigail and felt a surge of emotion race through her. Taking Abigail's hand into hers, she prayed that she'd wake so they could continue the chats they often had, but that was asking a lot.

Abigail had been brought to Dallas over a week ago, and since then she hadn't been conscious. For Madeleine it appeared as if she were dead. If it weren't for her chest rising and falling, she'd have thought it was so.

"Please, God, I don't ask for much, I really don't. Please make Abigail well; bring her back to me," Madeleine whispered, Abigail's hand in hers.

Over and over she prayed; so much she lost track of time.

A voice from the other room called, "Madeleine, where are you?"

Madeleine looked up. She knew she had to leave, but she didn't want to go.

The door to the bedroom cracked open. Madeleine's nanny stuck her head in and whispered, "There you are. You know you must let Miss Abigail rest."

"But—"

"No buts, leave her be," the nanny said.

Madeleine went to let Abigail's hand go, but just as she started to, Abigail grabbed it. Madeleine looked at her, shocked, and said, "Abby?"

"Maddy, hi," Abigail said, her voice cracking.

"Oh, Abby, you're awake, you're awake," Madeleine said as she lay on her.

Abigail yelped in pain from the weight being placed on her battered body.

Madeleine jumped up and said, "I'm sorry, I'm so sorry."

Abigail went to grab her instinctually with her right arm, but it was gone. Only the stump of what was remaining rose. "My arm?"

Madeleine looked at her with shock that she didn't know.

"My arm?" she again repeated in dismay.

"They had to…I'm so sorry. They had to remove it," Madeleine said, her voice cracking.

Abigail just stared at her stump, her expression showing the shock of the discovery.

"It was badly infected. They tried to save it, but they

couldn't without risking your life," Madeleine said, tears flowing down her cheeks.

"What am I going to do?" Abigail muttered as she thought about her career as a bounty hunter.

"I'm sure you'll be able to ride again, I'm sure of it," Madeleine said, hoping to cheer her up.

"I won't be able to…I can't shoot; my right was my dominant arm," Abigail said, her gaze not breaking from the bandaged stump.

"But you have your left," Madeleine said.

"You don't understand, I'm finished. How will I continue to work? What will I do?" Abigail said.

"I'm sure Mr. Dawson can find you a job somewhere, or maybe you can just take care of me full-time," Madeleine said. Mr. Dawson and his wife looked after Madeleine.

"But I'm not a nanny, I'm a bounty hunter; it's who I am," Abigail snapped, her temper beginning to rise. "Who had them cut my arm off?" she asked, turning her stare towards Madeleine.

Frightened by Abigail's intense gaze, Madeleine recoiled slightly and answered, "The doctor made the decision."

"Who brought me here? What happened?" she asked, her voice rising.

"You're scaring me," Madeleine cried.

"I don't care! What happened to me?" Abigail barked.

Madeleine jumped up and backed away from the bed.

"Where are you going? Answer my question," Abigail said.

"I'm going to go get Mr. Dawson," Madeleine said, fleeing the room.

In Madeleine's hurried departure, she didn't close the door. In the hall, Abigail could hear her talking to someone, but she couldn't tell who. Curious and in need of information, she tossed the sheet and blanket off her. She paused to make sure both her legs were there. After the discovery that her right arm had been taken, she just might find a leg missing too. Comforted to see both legs, she swung them off the mattress, only stopping when a searing jolt of pain shot up from her hip. The pain coursed its way up her spine, settling in the top of her head. She gasped but was determined to get answers. Bracing her body against the side of the mattress, she placed her feet firmly on the hardwood floor and pushed up with her left arm. After taking a moment to balance herself, she slowly shuffled her feet until she reached a large chest of drawers near the door.

The voices in the hall grew louder.

Abigail reached for the handle but was unable to grasp it as Mr. Dawson entered the room.

"Abby, what are you doing up?" he said, coming to her side.

Abigail held up her left hand and motioned for him to stop. "No, don't touch me; I don't need your help."

"But you're weak; you're still recovering from your injuries," Dawson said, standing back out of respect per her request.

"What happened to me?" she asked.

"I'll tell you, but you should lie down," a familiar voice came from the hall.

Abigail looked around the doorjamb to see Grady. "What are you doing here?"

"He brought you to us a week ago," Dawson answered.

Grady entered the room and said, "Good morning, Abby; how about you go lie down and I'll explain everything to you."

"How could you let them take my arm?" she asked, her eyes showing her anger towards a man she'd grown to trust.

"Please go lie down. I promise I'll explain it all," Grady said, reaching for her like Dawson had.

Abigail brushed off his hand and said, "I don't need your help, nor yours. I don't need anyone's help." She glared at them all, then slowly shuffled back to the bed and plopped down on the edge of it.

"What do you remember?" Grady asked.

"All of it. I remember getting shot in the arm, but that doesn't explain why you had them cut it off!" she roared.

"Abby, you don't remember everything clearly," Grady said.

"I do, I remember being shot and..." she said, pausing to think about what had happened next.

"And the blast struck your arm just above the elbow. You luckily were spared getting hit in the torso," Grady said, pausing as he recalled seeing the incident firsthand.

He sighed and continued, "Your arm was barely hanging on. You looked down at it then passed out. You lost a lot of blood. It's a miracle you're alive."

"I don't want to hear about miracles, I want my arm," Abigail hollered.

"I know you're upset," Grady said.

"Did you kill the bastard who did this?" she asked.

"I did," Grady replied.

"What happened with Thomas?" she asked, suddenly remembering him.

"He and his siblings are safe with family in Ohio," Grady answered.

"That's good news about the little ones," she said sweetly.

"Something positive out of all the tragedy, I suppose," he said.

"And Owen Blake?" she asked.

"I don't know. I heard there were bodily remains at the crater but nothing that could be identified," Grady replied.

"So only the children survived. So sad, what was it all for?"

"For them, if we hadn't…if you hadn't made us help them, they'd be dead too probably. You, Abigail, are something else, a true savior," Grady said, reaching for her hand.

She recoiled and asked, "What happened next, you brought me here?"

"I did. You were in bad shape. I took you to Perry, had you patched up; but you were in and out of consciousness and the pain was so bad they prescribed laudanum. Anytime you'd come to, you'd mumble something about Madeleine and coming to Dallas. I figured out how to contact them and made arrangements to bring you here. We arrived a week ago. Mr. Dawson immediately had a doctor, one of the best around, come pay a visit, and based upon the condition of your arm, he suggested it had to be removed. If he hadn't, it would have killed you."

"But of all people, you know I can't do what I do without my arm," she said.

Grady pulled a chair up, placed it next to her and sat. "There was no other option—your arm or your life. Trust me, Abby, your arm was done. It was shattered, the bone was destroyed, and it was never going to mend. When I got you here, the skin of the upper arm had turned black. You're lucky you didn't get sepsis and die. I don't know how else to put it; there was no other option."

Abigail began to weep. "What am I going to do?"

"Mr. Dawson told me just last night that he could use you in his office…" Grady replied. Mr. Dawson was an attorney and had a successful practice in Dallas.

Abigail interrupted him and blurted out, "Office? Do I look like someone who works in an office?"

"Abigail, you don't need to do anything. You're family; you can live with us. We will take care of you," Dawson said.

"I don't need anyone to take care of me. I can do it myself," she barked out of anger.

Madeleine stood behind Dawson, clinging to his

hand. She'd never seen Abigail bitter and angry before.

"What if we start training you to shoot with your left?" Grady asked.

Abigail glared at him and said, "A one-armed woman bounty hunter. The only thing correct about that is being a one-armed woman. My days of riding are done, finished."

Seeing there would be no way to overcome the initial shock she was going through, Grady got up and addressed the others. "Let's give her time."

"Go, leave," Abigail snapped.

Dawson, Madeleine and Grady exited the room.

When the door closed, Abigail began to weep as her anger turned to sorrow. What would her life be now? What would she do? She loved what she did because it gave her purpose and gave her the ability to make a difference. Just what would she be able to do now that could even come close? Drowning in her own self-pity, she fell back onto the pillows and stared at the ceiling. Suddenly a thought came to just end it all. If she couldn't ride and be what she wanted, why not just end it all? The thought was disturbing, yet there it was. Her mind then raced to the woman she'd killed back in Oklahoma and how that had made her feel. She'd wanted so desperately to save her, to show her that she had more to live for, but the woman was determined. Was this the emotion she was feeling now? Was losing her arm and losing the ability to be a bounty hunter the same as losing everything?

Abigail lost herself in deep reflection. The minutes

turned to hours, and before she knew it, the sun had lowered, leaving her in darkness.

A tap on the door broke her out of her thoughts. At first she ignored it, but the tap came again. "What?"

"It's me," Madeleine said sheepishly.

Abigail sighed.

"I wrote you something," Madeleine said.

"Just leave it," Abigail replied. She was still steeping in anger and didn't want to snap at Madeleine again, so she felt it best she leave whatever it was.

Madeleine slipped a note under the door and walked away.

Curious, Abigail rose, her body screaming in pain. Unable to see, she lit the lantern on the nightstand. Only having one arm made it harder, but she managed. Its orange glow illuminated the space. Slowly she got to her feet and, like earlier, shuffled to the door. On the floor she spotted the note. Leaning against the wall with her left arm, she used it to brace her weight as she squatted down. She only knew what Grady had told her, but her entire body felt like it had been run over by a wagon, not just her now missing arm. Using her knees to support her weight, she reached out with her hand and took the note. She sat back, unfolded it and read.

Dear Abigail,

I know you are angry, and I can understand. Losing something like your arm is difficult. If I could take the pain away, I would. I know you're also angry that you can't do what you've loved for so long, but one thing you told me long ago is that life shows up; it's up to us to accept it and move on.

I do that every time you leave, I accept it and move on, but for me it feels like I lose a part of me each time you go.

I love you so very much and have you solely to thank for saving me years ago. I know that your life will now look different, but I am here for you, as are Mr. and Mrs. Dawson and your friend Mr. Grady. Together we can do anything because we're a family.

Lastly, I pray that you stay. I know you may not, as you always have somewhere to go, but you can't stop a girl from hoping.

Love, Madeleine

It wasn't a long note, but the words written were poignant, straight to the point, and hit her with the force of a train at full speed. Tears welled up as she cast her eyes on the words a second time, this time letting them marinate in her mind.

Needing to see her, Abigail opened the door slightly. "Maddy!" Abigail called out.

"Yes!" Madeleine replied from farther down the hall. She stepped out and peeked down the hall towards the open door. "Abby, did you call my name?"

"Come here," Abigail said.

Madeleine didn't move. She replied, "Are you angry with me?"

"Oh no, not at all. I'm the opposite, I'm happy," Abigail answered sweetly.

Hearing that, Madeleine raced down the hall, pushed the door open, and stood looking down at Abigail. "You liked the note?"

"I loved it," Abigail said, holding up her hand.

Madeleine took her hand.

"Sit with me," Abigail said.

Doing as she was asked, Madeleine sat next to Abigail on the floor. "I wasn't sure if you'd get mad or not."

"How could I get mad? Your letter is beautiful," Abigail said, wiping a couple of tears from her cheeks.

"You're crying," Madeleine said. "I don't think I've ever seen you cry."

"Don't let anyone ever tell you they don't cry, everyone does," she said, again taking Madeleine's hand into hers.

"I'm so sorry you lost your arm," Madeleine said.

"I am too," Abigail replied.

"Can I ask you a question?" Madeleine asked.

"Of course, anything."

"Will you be staying?"

Abigail squeezed Madeleine's hand tightly and answered, "What you wrote. Using my words really affected me. It's so easy to give advice or comfort, but the thing is I believe in them. What I told you long ago is no different for me. Life showed up for you, and you accepted the change bravely. I look at the life you lived and how you've grown to become this amazing girl, so smart, wise, yet very sweet and empathetic. I can also learn from you, and the second time I read the words I told you, I decided that I'm going to have to accept what life has thrown at me. I may not have my right arm, but I have you, and guess what? I still have my left to hug you with," Abigail said.

"Does that mean you're staying?" Madeleine said, crying.

"Yes, I'm staying. My life is here with you," Abigail said.

Madeleine gently buried her head into Abigail's shoulder, being careful not to hit her stump.

Abigail gave her a kiss on the top of the head and said, "I love you, Madeleine."

"I love you, Abigail."

Grady heard them talking down the hall and shot a glance their way. Spotting the two embracing, a smile broke out across his face.

"What's happening?" Dawson asked, stepping up next to Grady.

"The first step in the healing process," Grady replied.

DALLAS, TEXAS

DECEMBER 24, 1893

Using her left hand, Abigail cocked her Colt and raised it. She stared down the sights to the bottle beyond and placed her index finger on the trigger. As she squeezed, she envisioned how the shot would go. She saw the hammer going forward and striking the casing of the round. She watched in slow motion as the bullet exited the barrel, spiraling towards the target and striking it perfectly, the bottle smashing into hundreds of pieces.

When the pistol did go off, it happened exactly as she'd seen it in her mind's eye. The bottle exploded in the distance followed by Madeleine cheering the shot.

"Yeah!" Madeleine squealed with joy.

"Not bad, not bad. My turn," Grady said, stepping forward.

Hitting the bottle felt good. It had been a while since she had shot, and because it was Christmas, she'd promised Madeleine they'd shoot.

Grady cocked his pistol, raised it, and seconds later fired. Like her, he struck a bottle. "Ha, one for one."

Abigail gave Madeleine a playful sneer, gazed down at the other four bottles, and asked, "Who has a watch?"

"What do you have in mind?" Grady asked, pulling his pocket watch from his vest pocket.

"When the second-hand hits twelve, tell me," she said.

Grady watched as the hand ticked around. "Now."

Abigail cocked the pistol, aimed and fired. The shot destroyed a bottle. However, this time she didn't stop at one. Still holding the pistol in the air, she maneuvered her thumb, cocked it again, firmly reasserted her grip, took aim and fired again, striking a second bottle. She repeated it twice, the other two shots hitting perfectly. "Time?"

"Thirteen seconds!" Grady exclaimed.

"Yeah, Abigail!" Madeleine cheered.

Abigail twirled the pistol on her finger and holstered it. She smiled and said, "I can do it in ten seconds."

"Ten?" Grady asked.

Looking at the shards of glass, Abigail replied, "Yeah, ten."

"Woman, that was impressive, and you did it wearing a skirt," Grady said, giving her a wink.

Since she'd been in Dallas, Abigail had been wearing more traditional clothing, mainly because she hadn't gotten around to getting any trousers that fit her yet.

"You did so well," Madeleine said happily, wrapping her arms around Abigail's waist.

"That wasn't bad. There's always room for improvement," she said.

"I think I can do it in nine seconds," Grady said arrogantly, teasing her.

The back door of the house opened. Dawson stepped onto the landing and hollered, "I have a telegram for Abby."

"Oh, a telegram, I'll go get it." Madeleine squealed with excitement and sprinted off. She promptly returned and said, "Can I read it to you, please?"

Abigail didn't need a second to think about it. "Of course you can read it to me."

Happily, Madeleine unfolded the paper and read out loud, "Dear Miss Abigail. My uncle is going to Dallas for a business trip just after the New Year, and he is taking me and my sister, Emma, with him. We've never been to Texas, so this will prove to be quite the adventure for us both. I am hoping you will be there when we are because I would so like to see you again. If you will be and would like to see us, please do reply to this telegram and tell us a good date for a social call. Your friend forever, Anna. P.S. If it's possible, I would love for you to teach me how to shoot a pistol."

Hearing those words from Anna warmed Abigail's heart. It had been a long time since she'd heard from Anna, and seeing her would make for a wonderful reunion.

"Who's Anna?" Grady asked.

"Abigail saved her and her sister as well as other girls from a group of bad men," Madeleine blurted out.

"How am I not surprised?" Grady said, laughing. "Always the hero and savior."

"What do I always say?" she asked Grady.

"It's what you do," he quipped.

"It will be nice seeing Anna again. You'll like her a lot, Madeleine. You two will get along famously," Abigail said, caressing the top of Madeleine's head.

"I look forward to meeting her finally," Madeleine said. "You should reply right away."

"I will, don't you worry, but first I need to show

Grady how lefties shoot," she joked. "What was the time you said, nine seconds?"

"Yep, nine seconds. Do you doubt me?" he replied.

"Come to think of it, I think I can do it in eight seconds," she said.

"Eight? Wanna bet?" he asked.

"I don't want to take your hard-earned money; that wouldn't be fair. But I will happily enjoy the bragging rights. Now go set them up, cowboy; it's time I show you what I'm capable of," Abigail teased.

THE END

ABOUT THE AUTHOR

G. Michael Hopf is the best-selling author of acclaimed series, THE NEW WORLD and other novels. He spent two decades living a life of adventure before he settled down and became a novelist full time. He is a combat veteran of the Marine Corps and a former executive protection agent.

He lives with his family in San Diego, CA

Please feel free to contact him at geoff@gmichaelhopf.com with any questions or comments.

www.gmichaelhopf.com

www.facebook.com/gmichaelhopf

PRAIRIE JUSTICE

Books by G. MICHAEL HOPF

THE NEW WORLD SERIES

THE END
THE LONG ROAD
SANCTUARY
THE LINE OF DEPARTURE
BLOOD, SWEAT & TEARS
THE RAZOR'S EDGE
THOSE WHO REMAIN

THE NEW WORLD SERIES SPIN OFFS

NEMESIS: INCEPTION
EXIT

THE WANDERER SERIES

VENGEANCE ROAD
BLOOD GOLD
TORN ALLEGIANCE

THE BOUNTY HUNTER SERIES

LAST RIDE
THE LOST ONES
PRAIRIE JUSTICE

ADDITIONAL BOOKS

HOPE with A. American
DAY OF RECKONING
DETOUR: A POST-APOCALYTPIC HORROR STORY
DRIVER 8: A POST-APOCALYPTIC NOVEL
THE DEATH TRILOGY with John W. Vance

Made in the USA
Monee, IL
03 December 2019